IT'S COMPLICATED

BELLA FONTAINE

KHARDINE GRAY

The following story contains mature themes, strong language.

IT'S COMPLICATED

USA Today Bestselling Author

Khardine Gray

Writing as

Bella Fontaine

CHAPTER 1

Patterson

"Pat, get up," came that voice again.

I moved my head to the side and snuggled closer into the bed sheets. That was all anyone was getting out of me today.

Damn, was I tired. I couldn't remember why, and I didn't want to.

All I knew was, my bed felt extra comfy and I wasn't leaving it.

"Pat!!" The voice said with more insistence.

A woman.

The voice belonged to a woman.

I was too tired to figure out which one it could be, but it made me snap my eyes open a little too quickly. I wasn't prepared for the bright morning sunlight that pierced through the blinds and felt like knives piercing through my eyes.

God, what the hell?

How was it morning already? It seemed like just minutes ago that I'd closed my eyes. Maybe it was.

Footsteps sounded in the corridor then in the room.

"Pat, get the hell up."

Pat...

It was Georgie, my PA. She was the only one who insisted on calling me Pat. Her abbreviation for my actual name, Patterson. She said Patterson was a surname, and since calling me by my surname, which was Flynn, seemed rude and would be weird at the office, she didn't want to call me Flynn either.

Instead she chose Pat, which in many books was a woman's name.

I couldn't remember why she was here again. Granted, it wouldn't have been that unusual for my wonderful secretary to be at my penthouse suite, or... in my bed.

No, it wasn't like that. We didn't have the relationship most people assumed we had. We weren't sleeping together.

We had a sort of weird unconventional relationship that just worked for us.

I lifted my head as she stomped over to me and tossed a white button-up shirt on the duvet. She then loomed over me and scowled.

The sunlight caught the beautiful light brown of her eyes and radiated off her dark skin, reminding me of raw honey. The kind Mom used to get from my uncle before he moved to Barcelona to expand his business.

Better to focus on Georgie's ethereal beauty than try to figure out why she could be mad at me.

"Pat, don't let me get the water. I mean it. I will grab that bucket and toss ice cold water all over you." She wagged her pointer at me and straightened.

I simply groaned and gave her a haggard stare. "Woman, why are you so mean? Can't you see I'm on my last lap? I'm so tired."

"Don't you 'woman' me, Pat." She folded her arms under her breasts. I just noticed she was wearing one of my shirts. "You have to be at the office in an hour for the meeting. I told you not to go out last night. You got in at four. Was she really that good for you to stay out all damn night?"

"I can't remember." That meant I'd been drinking. Drinking a lot if I couldn't remember shit from last night.

Hold on... something was coming to me.

I was playing *Call of Duty* with Georgie. That was how we usually ended a hard day at the office.

Most nights saw us hanging out together, playing some video game on my Xbox. Five years ago, when we met, that was how we connected. Games. I'd never met many girl/ woman gamers, and the fact that talking to her was like talking to a guy didn't hurt either. That was how we began and blossomed into this relationship or attachment. Whatever it was. It worked.

During our break last night, I went out to get some more snacks at the convenience store. I ran into Phoebe there, one of my hookups, and then I sent Georgie a message letting her know I'd be back later.

Phoebe and I then headed to her place. I remembered a lot of wine. Me pouring it over her naked body.

That was it.

I couldn't remember how I got back here.

"Look, forget it. We don't have time for shit like this. You can't be late for your meeting. Your dad made me promise to get you there on time."

Ugh. I didn't know what the hell my old man would want to see me about.

Everything was all clear cut.

He was retiring from the company in three months and handing the place over to me.

Simple.

Flynn Property Development Inc. would be mine,

and I'd live the dream of owning the multi-billion-dollar international corporation.

Happiness. That was happiness from achieving a life-long goal.

Dad had groomed me from birth to take over the company. I was his only child, and because of that I had everything the man could give.

I was thirty-six and the perpetual bachelor. The billionaire playboy who had no plans to be anything other than that. I was damn good at my job and a guy who was living his best life.

"Baby, I'm not going to work today. How about we blow the day off and go to the beach? Sailing? You love that. It'll be a great day." I nodded.

She must have been pissed at how I'd ditched her in the middle of a game because she scowled at me.

"Pat, I don't consider spending my time on the yacht serving you drinks with some skanky chick you picked up as a great day." Georgie tapped her foot and shook her head at me. She actually looked upset.

"When did I do that?" I frowned and sat upright.

"*Last time.* If you're taking me sailing, you take just me sailing. Not under some guise, and then I end up being your servant for the day. No thank you."

"Baby—"

"Don't 'baby' me either. I'm serious, Pat. You have to be at the office in less than an hour now. I may be your

PA, but your dad's my boss, and I still answer to him. He wants you at the office nine a.m. sharp. He has another meeting straight after you, and he needs to speak to you about important stuff."

I tilted my head to the side, and a lock of hair fell over my eye.

Important stuff. What the hell did that mean? He didn't mention anything about important stuff before. Clearly, he'd spoken to her away from me. Also, this version of her was very rare. Her trying to get me to the office for a simple meeting with Dad.

"When did you speak to him?"

Her frown deepened. "I told you. It was just before I got here last night. He called me on my way over. You were texting Mandy, and I asked you if you were listening, and you said yes."

Fuck.

I wasn't listening. How would I have heard that when Mandy was sending me naked pictures of her tits? She'd just had implants to make them bigger than they already were and wanted my opinion.

I was a man. Wave a pair of perfect tits at me, and all brain function and senses would leave me.

This time, it would have been better if I'd been listening because had I truly heard her, I would have called Dad last night.

"Okay, I'm getting up. You might not want to be in

here for this part. Not unless you want to see me in my birthday suit." I was butt naked.

Her mouth dropped. "Pat, I was in here sleeping when you got in this morning. You got in bed naked with me?" Her voice took on a shrill tone, and her eyes widened.

I laughed. "Georgie, all I know right now is, I'm naked and I'm here. I can't remember how I got here, but I assure you I would have kept on my boxers had I seen you in the bed."

She picked up a pillow and hit me with it several times.

"How can you not see me? I'm not four feet tall."

"Five feet and two inches. God made the honey-colored woman short, but she has a tall personality." I was simply reiterating what she'd said to me many times.

I was six feet four. She was like a dwarf when she stood next to me.

Yes, I should have seen her in the bed, but I didn't.

"I can't with you today, Pat. You drive me crazy."

"Maybe it's because I'm so used to sleeping with you." I opened my palms.

"*Jesus*, please don't let anyone hear you say that. The whole office already thinks I'm sleeping with you." She opened my wardrobe and tossed me a tie.

"You are sleeping with me," I teased.

7

"Stop it." She pouted. The long ends of her ponytail bobbled as she cut me a glance over her shoulder.

"It's hardly the worst thing in the world."

She threw me a pair of pants and shrugged into a pair of yoga pants that were draped over a chair on the other side of the room. She then grabbed her purse. I noticed she kept on my shirt.

"Georgie, you know if you leave the place dressed in my clothes, it's a dead giveaway that something's going on between us."

She stopped by the door and looked over at me. "Today, I don't care. I have to get back to my place and change. I overslept, and my stuff here is just… not."

"Wait… so what time are you getting to work?" I thought we'd be going in together like most days.

It would have been nice to have the support today since it looked like Dad had something up his sleeves.

"After lunch. I've asked Sally to take care of the phone."

After lunch...

I narrowed my eyes at her. It wasn't often that she took half days, and if she was taking all that time off, where was she going?

"What are you up to, baby?"

"Stuff," she answered simply, which meant she was up to something she didn't want to share with me just yet. Secretive. Last time she got like that was on my birthday. She and my best friend, Ivan, planned a surprise party for me. Since my birthday wasn't for another four months, I doubted it was that, and she wouldn't have organized a party like that again.

She got this guarded look in her eyes and gave me a one-shoulder sassy shrug.

"I'll see you at the office. Don't let me down, Pat. Get there by nine, or I won't speak to you ever again."

I brought my fingers up to my lips, kissed my forefinger, and saluted her.

This woman knew exactly what to say to me to make me do whatever she wanted.

I might have been the biggest asshole on this side of the planet, but letting her down was something I'd never do.

She smiled at me and shook her head. At least I'd managed to break down her annoyance on some level.

I just wondered what stuff she was tending to that would keep her busy all morning.

Close as we were, there was a line I never crossed when she decided to put up her fence and remind me our relationship was professional. I was her boss, and she was my PA.

While she kept some aspects of her life private, I spilled the tea on mine every chance I got.

It wasn't her fault that I told her everything.

CHAPTER 2

Patterson

OKAY, I was here.

I got myself here and in one piece.

As usual, I got the once-over looks I normally received from women as I walked out of the parking lot and in through the revolving doors of Flynn's.

I'd always loved attention and was guilty of doing my best to keep that attention.

Like now. There was a sexy blond woman coming out of the ladies' room. Looked a little like Amanda Seyfried. She looked at me, and I didn't just look back at her.

I made sure she knew I thought she was gorgeous by stopping mid-stride to look her up and down. Then I nodded my approval, smiled, and winked at her as I continued to Dad's office.

She was number worthy, but it was five minutes to nine, and I would definitely be late if I stopped to chat.

I was anxious and eager to see what Dad wanted to see me about, and truthfully, a little nervous. It was the way Georgie was acting.

I never really had much to be nervous about when it came to work, but there was always the possibility of something happening. I didn't know what that would be, but today felt like something was on the horizon, or in the making.

I hated surprises, which was why when Georgie and Ivan planned that party for me, they went through all manners of covert missions to pull it off without me having an inkling about what they were up to.

I'd worked here since I graduated high school. I earned my business degree at UCLA just to have that backing, like most of the Flynn men in our family. I also didn't want to feel like any of my cousins had anything on me, or over me.

In addition to this branch here in L.A., which was the headquarters, the company had branches in New York, Chicago, Miami, and Atlanta. That was this side of the globe. We also had branches in every major city of the world. Each run by family members. Dad would say I had the privilege of belonging to a large family. I would say otherwise because most of my cousins were complete pricks who hated that I'd be getting the company when Dad retired.

Those fuckers would take any opportunity to steal the chance from me because they always had one thing or another to say about me.

However, fact and figures spoke for themselves. I never came across a deal that I couldn't close, and I always found new businesses.

I loved to play hard because I worked damn hard, and Dad knew that. As long as he knew that, I didn't care about anybody else.

Just my dad. Head boss until I was boss.

When I entered his office, he straightened behind his desk and motioned his hand toward the chair in front of him for me to sit.

He wore a crude expression on his face that made him look his age. Dad was seventy. Seventy with a thick head of dark hair like mine, with the exception of the silver streaks on the sides that made him look like Mr. Fantastic.

He furrowed his thick brows and glared at me. That was it. No 'Good morning,' no 'How are you,' no anything like that.

He just had that gruff expression on his face, and I knew something was definitely up.

"Hey, Dad, are you okay? You look like you forgot to take your blood pressure medicine this morning." I was going for lighthearted. Something to ease the tension in the room, but it didn't work.

He glanced toward the Monet painting next to the floor-to-ceiling windows, and his frown deepened.

When he looked back to me, he pulled in a shallow breath and reached into his drawer to pull out some newspapers and a few copies of the *National Enquirer*.

He stood and dropped the newspapers down on the desk space in front of me.

It was today's paper. The L.A. Times. On the front cover was a picture of me with Adriana, a Victoria's Secret model I'd hooked up with the night before last.

The headline read:

Billionaire Playboys. What is the future of Flynn's Property Development Inc.?

Dad moved the paper aside so I could see the other one underneath. That was *The Chronicle*.

I was on the front cover of that too. This one was not as civil as the L.A. Times.

There was a picture of me walking with a topless Adriana up to the penthouse. They'd blurred out her tits, but people got the drift of what we were up to.

Dad threw down the fucking *National Enquirer* and flipped to page two.

While I wasn't on the front cover on the magazine, they showed a naked Adriana, with me kissing her against my car in the parking lot at the penthouse.

Fuck, it was like I had no privacy whatsoever.

Okay... I knew I'd landed myself in this mess by kissing and practically ravishing a naked woman outside for all to see, but I was being followed. That part wasn't on. Not in the least.

"Dad—"

He held up his hand and cut me off.

He cut me off and glared at me. "I'm tired of this. I'm really tired of this. The papers called me yesterday, and I managed to stop a majority of them printing this shit, but these fought me on it. I thought, you know what? I can't keep covering your shit up. I'm too old to be cleaning up after you like you're a kid."

My father was the kind of guy who was very well put together and decent. He did not curse unless he was seething. Even then he limited it. He'd always said it was his way of being an example to me. That never actually worked because saying *fuck* was part of my every-hour vocabulary.

I did, however, snap to attention when my old man was mad, and today he looked like he was mad as hell with me.

"Dad, this is bullshit. I can't help that the paparazzi follow me. They just wait for me to slip up so they can post this stuff about me."

"Patterson, you make this company look bad. You tarnish our name with your behavior. We have a name to uphold that has been around for generations, and you're supposed to be the next head of this empire. You're not just taking over the business in L.A. You're taking over everywhere, and you don't take anything seriously. You're thirty-six, and you don't even act like a twenty-six-year-old who wants this opportunity."

His eyes bore into mine.

"Look, I'm sorry. I'll make sure the next time I pick up a woman, we get up to our badness inside my house." I don't know who told me to say that.

I shouldn't have.

People said I got my humor from my granddad. It skipped a generation when it leapt over Dad and got me instead. The humor and the thirst for women. It was that Italian blood in my veins. Grandfather had been married eight times before he died two years ago.

Hell, he met the good Lord after saying 'I Do' the day before he died. I thought, though, that he must have died in the night while trying to get it up for his new bride, who was twenty-five.

The same new bride who'd tried to get his whole fortune. Unfortunately, Grandfather didn't have the instinct it took to know that the only reason a twenty-five-year-old would marry a ninety-year-old was money.

"Things have to change, son. It's come to a point where things have to change." Dad straightened.

"Like how?"

"I've tried my best not to interfere in your life and let you live it, but before I retire, I have to fulfill my last act as head of this company. The family were against me for making you an equal partner in the business. I fought them on it because you do a damn good job. But this isn't just about doing a good job. There's more to it than that. So much more, and so much more that I want for you."

God, Lord... where was this going?

I didn't like the direction this conversation was taking. It was just going left, left, left, no matter what I did and said to bring it back.

"Dad, I think you're overreacting because of a few pictures. The papers are always on my ass about one thing or another."

"Yes, you know why, son? You're an eligible bachelor. The playboy billionaire who hooks up with the most beautiful woman he can find, and not just any random woman either. They're all models and celebs."

I looked at him, trying to figure out why that was so

bad. "You want me to hook up with women who are not that?"

I didn't call women ugly. That wasn't me. I just thought each had a different kind of beauty. If I didn't find a woman attractive, then that was on me, not because she wasn't beautiful. That was part of my own special code.

"Patterson, I want you to settle down and stop this nonsense."

"My private life is mine. Not even you have the right to tell me what to do with my life or who I should be with."

"Well, I thought so too, and I respected that until shit got real and I realized I wasn't going to be taking care of this company anymore. Realistically, I should have retired five years ago. I stayed on because I enjoy my work. But it's time for me to go. I don't want to retire knowing that I left this place to you to run into the ground."

My mouth fell open. Was that what he seriously thought? "Dad, you're wrong to say that to me. Come on. You know how much I care about the place."

"You care, but this behavior is not acceptable. All your cousins act in a respectable way. They all have families and act professionally and in line with the sophisticated manner we uphold in this company. I've just been around carrying the name and carrying you too. The loose women have to go, son."

"Why is this a conversation we're having at work?" It just dawned on me that this wasn't the ordinary type of thing we'd discuss here. It wasn't the first time he'd brought up his disapproval of my love for changing women like I changed clothes.

It was the first time that he'd brought it up *here* though. Here at work. It wasn't that deep. I understood the need to chew me out over the articles in the paper. I agreed it was bad and not one of my finest moments. I did make the company look a certain type of way, which admittedly wasn't in the best light.

This conversation, however, was not work related.

It was bordering on something else, probably the something I had a nagging feeling about because it was going so far left, I couldn't get a handle on it.

Then there was the look that washed over Dad's face.

"The investors are concerned."

"Then fuck them. Whoever doesn't like me can jump ship and leave. We don't need their money."

We didn't. Those miserable bastards, the lot of them, just invested in us to get a piece of the pie. Dad was the generous type and wanted to share his wealth. I'd already started making a list of who I'd be getting rid of once I took over.

"Was it Briony?" I narrowed my eyes at him. Briony was a lead investor. The type of woman who was always at the Hamptons or on some spa break. That woman hated me because I'd dumped her daughter.

Just like the mother, the daughter was crazy and clingy. We went on one date. I never even made it to the bedroom with her because the woman started talking about children. That was the warning sign to stay far away and protect my sperm.

One date, and she told everyone how I broke her heart and took advantage of her. One date, and she went to the papers telling them I was the father of her baby. I made sure I didn't have a night like last night, and the situation went as far as me doing a paternity test when said child was born.

Of course, it wasn't mine and she made herself look stupid, but she'd dragged my name through the dirt with that. If that were happening now, I would probably understand the need for this conversation.

"She was one of them," Dad confessed. "However, she wasn't the only one. They're thinking of pulling their investments, and I'm banking on that for the Miami beach project. Just because of the size of the project."

"You know, I almost thought this meeting was going to be about that." Of course, I would, since I was the one who'd secured the deal to build a five-star luxury resort near the beach in the space that was now a land-fill. The owners were selling, and I'd snapped up the land.

Prior to the sale, the land was said to have traces of lead. The reports were, however, wrong. The land was cheap for that reason. It was near the beach with a paradise view. I got in there fast and bought it while it was still cheap. Of course, though, like with everything, the money I used wasn't truly considered mine when I purchased under the umbrella of the company.

It was company property. Company idea. And if I wanted to fulfill the vision I saw for the place, I had to carry out all work under the company jurisdiction. It hadn't been a worry, until now.

"Patterson, I can't allow you to work on that project, or any other for the matter, until I know you're serious. I need a man in charge of the place, not a boy, and definitely not a playboy."

My stomach tightened along with my chest.

What was he saying to me?

"Dad… what specifically are you saying?" I had to give him a cold, hard stare because he couldn't be saying what it sounded like he was saying.

"I'm going to be real with you and make a stand I should have made years ago when you first started working here. I hoped you'd grow out of these immature ways, but you just grew into a brat. A man who didn't really grow up because he'd lived a spoilt, charmed, cushy lifestyle. I need to leave someone serious in charge, and I'm giving you a chance to show me that is you."

"Giving me a chance?" I didn't realize this was about chance. Unless I'd just taken a turn into *The Twilight Zone* and he was about to tell me he had another son I didn't know about, I was his only son. I came to work here believing the place would be mine one day.

I'd been here for close to twenty years in one way or another. Work experience, my internship, and climbing the ranks to where I was today.

Now, I was being told I was going to get a chance to show how serious I was.

"I was under the impression that I already displayed how seriously I take this company," I added.

"Well, if you think that, you're about to get a rude awakening. I'm done with scandalous reports and articles like these." He pointed to the papers on the desk. "Women are your problem. Loose women who encourage this sort of trash. You're thirty-six. All your cousins are married and settled down. Just like I was when I first took over the company. If you love women so much, find one. *A* woman. One woman. A woman who's marriage material. Not just a side piece or a fling.

I want you to find a woman you will be marrying before my retirement. That is the only way I'm handing anything over to you."

What kind of a motherfucking hell dimension had I walked into this morning?

"What the hell did you just say to me?" I had to stand up now.

No way was he serious.

"You heard me."

"I think I heard you. I just can't be certain the bullshit I just heard was really you talking."

"Patterson—"

Now it was my turn to interrupt. I held up my hand. "You think this is right? What part of that request seems okay to you? Please tell me which part?"

He released a sigh of frustration. It should have been me who looked frustrated. I'd, however, skipped past frustrated and landed on infernal mad.

"Patterson, it may sound farfetched, but it isn't. When I met your mother, I knew from the first moment I saw her that I was going to marry her. Times were simpler then. None of this technical stuff. In fact, it isn't even about the times. All you have to do is look for the kind of woman you'd want to be with for the rest of your life. It really is as simple as that. Your mother and I were engaged two weeks after we met, and we've been together for fifty beautiful years I wouldn't trade for anything in this world."

All I could do was look at him.

Nice as it was to hear him talk that way about Mom, I wasn't like him in that respect.

I thought the fact that I was thirty-six years old, had never had a long-term girlfriend, and was always with the type of women who were just playmates said everything.

It should have. In my head it said I wasn't that guy. Not the dating type, not the relationship type, not anything more than fun type.

The women I hooked up with knew that about me straight off the bat, and if I saw them acting in a way they looked like they expected more from me, I ended it.

That was me, up front and straight to the point. You couldn't be disappointed if I never gave you anything to hope for.

This was an outrage. A complete outrage.

"Dad, I respect you. I do. I respect you, and I'm grateful for all that you and Mom have done for me, but this is wrong, and you know it."

"So, you're saying you won't do it?" He eyed me quizzically.

"I'm saying I'll talk to you when you come to your senses. This isn't business, Dad. This is you trying to impose shit on me. Your own ideology of what you want me to be when you know damn straight that I'm the real deal here. Nobody can do what I do. Nobody."

"That right?"

I couldn't believe he would say that. It was like he'd gone blind and stupid.

"Dad, you know what I do for this place. I'll come back and speak to you when you remember." I stepped past him to head to the door.

"Hudson will be here next Friday," Dad blurted, stopping me in my tracks.

I turned around to face him, my face contorted. "Hudson? As in *Hudson?*"

Hudson, my asshole cousin who ran the New York and Chicago branches of the company.

Dad nodded. "We've been talking. For a while. He'll be here next Friday. I'm not messing around, Patterson. This is serious. What I said might sound outrageous to you, but that's what I want from you. I'll give you a chance to cool off and come and speak to me properly at the house tomorrow at lunchtime. If you want my exact stipulations, come. If you don't, then if you choose to remain working here, it will be as an employee under Hudson's direction if he wants to keep you on."

This was the kind of situation to drive a person

crazy. I couldn't believe it. I couldn't believe the madness of all of this.

Dad was serious.

I turned and walked out, not answering one way or the other.

Not knowing what I was going to do.

CHAPTER 3

Georgie

GOD, I was so happy I wasn't late.

Jesus. I couldn't even believe I took the risk, but like everything with Pat, once I got around that man, even my top priorities got pushed to the back.

That was saying something because I was a woman who always knew what she was doing and knew where I had to be. Never late, not even tardy, always reliable. That was me.

Recently, though, I'd been feeling bad. More like guilty. Guilty because it was looking like my life was finally about to take the direction I wanted it to take, and that meant leaving Pat.

God, that man drove me batshit crazy. He drove me crazy, and possibly more than that, whatever that more was. That was what he did to me. But he was good to me, and he was a friend.

A close friend I knew I had a seriously weird relationship with, which was highlighted this morning when I woke up next to him and realized I'd not only slept through my alarm but also that I could be late for my own very important meeting.

The waking up next to him this morning struck me more than usual today for the simple fact that today was the day when things could all change for me.

I made my way through the restaurant, heels click-clacking on the marble floors.

I'd dressed the part for the deal I wanted to secure with the client who could be my game changer.

There she was.

Marsha Marnel, owner of Fabulous Sports Wear, a seriously trendy sports store that had opened up in Santa Monica last year. She catered to the plus-size woman. Her mission statement was that a majority of exercise clothes were all geared toward thin women and women who already looked like they worked out. So, she created her own line of clothing to service women who she felt were left out. I thought it was fantastic and she was a nice person who I'd gotten on with straight away. Then, as if she wasn't nice enough, she also started a charity for women who'd been affected by domestic violence. This month, fifty percent of her sales were going to the charity.

She smiled when she saw me.

That had to be a good sign, right?

My nerves scattered at the prospect. I knew I practically had this in the bag, but damn, I was nervous as all hell. The kind of nerves that made me want to call Pat so he could calm me down in his own crazy way; except I couldn't do that because he didn't know about this.

He didn't know about this part of my life because I purposely kept him out.

I told Lana, my best friend, just for the fact that we were more like sisters than friends. Pat, on the other hand, was different. He was a different kind of best friend. But my boss at the end of the day.

Dad told me, more like cautioned me, that no matter what happened, I should always remember things like that, remember who people were.

When it came down to it, business was business.

That was what I was looking after now.

I made my way over to Marsha, who stood and put out her hand to shake mine in that gracious way she always did. She looked completely classy, as classy as this place.

Chez Moi was known for being classy. I'd only been here once before when I dated the Gladiators linebacker Ty Wilson. That was a great date. We didn't work out because that kind of spotlight lifestyle wasn't me, but I still appreciated that the man had treated me like a queen. It would be nice to have another good memory here.

"I hope I didn't keep you waiting too long." I smiled and sat once she had.

I wasn't late, and another one of my father's wisdoms was to never apologize for anything you haven't done. It made you look weak and gave the impression that you could be controlled.

My father was a very wise man.

"No, not at all." Marsha shook her head. "I got here early and grabbed a glass of wine. I'm terrible. I love any kind of French wine. The older, the better."

She laughed, and I did too. I loved wine just as much as the next person and planned to be celebrating with a bottle if she agreed to sign with my agency.

The thought got to me again. I wanted this so bad. Too bad, and so much I ached for it.

"I understand what you mean. I'm a wine girl. I hope to go to Italy next year to see the vineyards and visit Verona. Juliet's house," I bubbled. There was no harm in making small talk.

It sweetened the deal.

"Ahhh, beautiful. I've been many times." She nodded, and the ends of her blond hair bounced.

Small talk was great but I was eager to get to business. I just wanted to know if this was going to happen. Last year, I took the plunge to invest a few thousand dollars in setting up my long-awaited business. I called my company Vision Marketing and Advertising Consultancy, with the mission statement of creating the vision dreams were made of.

Seeing that things were starting to settle down with my horrible debt situation, and that Dad was starting to get better I took that leap of faith.

Progress was slow because I didn't have any clients then. Ty had put out a good word for me. We might not have lasted, but he'd helped me massively with a deal that started bringing in four figures a month. Sometimes three, but I was cool with that. It was a foundation.

I now had ten clients. Five of which were long term, and I managed their campaigns for them. I did all of that on the side while I worked for Pat. That was another thing he didn't know about.

Today, if Marsha signed with me, I'd be bringing in six figures a month. That would be enough money to get Dad a new place, pay all his medical bills, and damn, start me up properly. I was literally set up in my house, and I had a web designer who helped me out. Lana helped me with scheduling for my digital marketing campaigns in her spare time, and I had an à la carte virtual PA who did a few admin jobs for me.

There was a place on Santa Monica Blvd that I was eyeing up, and if Marsha said yes, I could at least go check it out.

She sighed and looked at me. The look held an air of the shift in her mood.

Damn...

I wished I didn't feel that wave of negativity that rocked my soul.

It was more of a thought that shimmied down to the pit of my stomach and somehow, I knew she didn't have good news for me.

"Georgia," she began. It was weird hearing her call me by my actual name. Everyone called me Georgie. "It's very hard for me to say this to you because I feel your passion for what you do."

"Oh... Did something happen?" I straightened and tried to swallow past the lump in my throat.

"Yes. I had a call from Nike yesterday. They want to invest in my business and my vision. They offered me a deal I couldn't turn away. It would have been very foolish of me to do so because they will more than put me on the map. I know it seems like all I'm doing is selling clothes, but I'm also selling a vision to a group of women who sometimes feel left out. They sometimes feel like they should cover their bodies because there's nothing for them in the stores. Nike want to run their own campaign, and I won't have to pay a cent. That is the only reason why I've decided not to sign with you."

Lord, have mercy. It was hard not to be sad about my loss when she'd just told me wonderful news. News that was wonderful for her but meant shit for me.

"I think it's amazing that they offered you such a deal. Congratulations." I nodded. Always gracious. That was me.

"Thank you. I'm truly sorry. I can't express how sorry I am, and I feel like I wasted your time because you drew up that wonderful plan for me that was so dynamic. I can't use it."

"No, no. We all have to do what's best for business."

Gracious again... And humble...

All that stuff that was supposed to make a nice person. I strived to be that, but sometimes I wished I were more of a bitch. Those people always got what they wanted.

I wasn't a pushover, but shit, it felt like over the last few years, I'd had to roll over and take whatever life threw at me.

Every time I hoped for something and it felt like things were going to work out, they didn't. They didn't work out, and I never saw it coming.

"Thank you, Georgia. I do wish you the best. Will you at least stay and have a glass of wine with me?"

I couldn't say no even though what I really wanted to do was go somewhere and lick my wounds in private.

Maybe cry a little.

"Of course. Let's drink to success." I nodded. "I know you're going to do amazing."

I wished I could say the same for myself.

"Thank you so, so much. Here's to our success and strong women who are entrepreneurs."

Right. That was completely correct for her.

Not so much for me.

CHAPTER 4

Georgie

LANA TOOK time out of her seriously busy schedule to come and see me for lunch.

My best friend looked like she'd just stepped off the cover of *Vogue*. Just like one of the models who wore her designs.

Lana was a fashion designer, and I was proud to say she worked for Dior. I was actually very proud to tell everyone that.

We'd known each other since college, and she'd had the dream of being some big designer in the city. My mom left us when I was ten. Dad had me and my older sister, Angelica, to take care of. We went through a rough time, but Lana had a rough life.

When Lana was nineteen, her mother killed herself. It was understandable that she didn't talk about it much.

Every time something negative happened to me, I tried to think of how strong she was.

I was doing it now, much as it wasn't particularly working.

"Hey, hunni." She smiled, waltzing in. Her bright brown eyes beamed as she stretched out her arms to either side to give me a hug.

I got up from the seat I'd planted myself in for the last half an hour.

We were in a little café near her workplace called Jake's Spot. From time to time, we met here for the awesome cinnamon pretzels and hot chocolate they made.

It wasn't as glamourous as Chez Moi, but this place was what you called homely with that good old feel atmosphere that soothed the soul. It was also the kind of place everyone came to. Rich, poor, the professional, and the laid-back.

I gave her a hug and rested against her chest, gathering strength and comfort as she patted my back.

"Hey." I sighed.

We pulled apart, but she didn't let me go just yet.

She gave me a pensive look, eyeing me sharply with her beautifully made-up eyes. Today, she wore an electric blue eyeshadow the same color as her top, which was striking against her dark skin.

"Girl, you can't let this get to you. No, no. Remember what I always say about closed doors?"

I released a breath and put my hand to my head. "When the door closes, you weren't meant to go in."

I repeated the words she'd said to me many times. For me, it felt like too many times. This time felt like the straw that would break my back.

"Remember that, Georgie. I don't say these things for nothing." She nodded.

We sat down opposite each other.

"Talk to me, tell me what you're thinking." She reached out and took my hand.

"I just really thought I'd get this client. I can't even be mad at her because she got the deal of a lifetime." I was trying hard not to cry, and I didn't want to cry here. Not here in front of people.

Then I'd also be a mess for work. Pat had already messaged me about him working from home. That meant I needed to reschedule all his appointments he had today for later in the week.

"Forget her in this mix. Tell me what your plan B is. You always think up something."

I shook my head. That was how disheartened I was.

I hadn't thought up anything as a plan B. Not like I usually did.

"Not this time. I can't think of anything. I'm stuck in a sea of big marketing companies that will swallow people like me right up. Marsha was that once-in-a-lifetime opportunity you get and you know you have to seize the moment and not mess up."

It was her who had contacted me. When I got her call, I was so blown away that I cried because of all it could mean for me.

"She wasn't your once-in-a-lifetime opportunity. Those don't work out like this. No, ma'am. We need to think up something else to help you to get to where you want to be."

I rested my hand down on the table and stared at the deep grooves in the wooden tabletop.

I was tired. Tired of everything. It just felt like too many years of me trying to get back to where I wanted to be. Of what I was once before.

My fear was that that time in my life was it. The only chance I'd get.

I'd studied marketing and advertising as a degree. I was completely passionate about it, and my goal was to run my own agency. I did everything I was supposed to do to be what they called highly desirable. It was one of those careers were there were so many of us that you needed to do different things to stand out.

I'd worked for some amazing companies. Did my internship in New York and stayed there for years after college. I was saving up for my own business. Then Dad got sick.

Dad got sick in the worst way possible and never told me how bad things were. I got a call one day letting me know he'd had a stroke and the stroke was related to his poor heart condition. We'd lived in L.A. all my life, and I'd left him to live my dream.

I came back to find he'd lost everything. His health, our family home, and all the savings.

How?

My sister. My sister, who damaged everything she touched. My sister, who'd abandoned us the same way Mom did and never looked back when Dad needed her.

She was supposed to be my big sister, but it was me who had to step up my game and be the adult. I had to make sacrifices. I had to give up everything. She was wherever she was living it up, and I was here just trying to survive.

Lana gave my hand a gentle squeeze.

"Georgie, sometimes we have to step away from our comfort zone to make certain things happen. I know you want this badly, and I'll do my best to spread the word. Have you thought of maybe just getting back into the marketing world as a job, I mean?"

I blinked and focused on her. That was a really good

idea, but I didn't just want to leave Pat. To me it had to be for this reason. Working for myself. Working for me and making myself flourish.

He paid me well, and I was pretty much free to do whatever I wanted as long as I did everything else he wanted.

Things like today, for example, would have been harder to pull off if I worked for someone else. It was after lunch, and if I didn't show up today at work, I'd still get paid for the day. I didn't know anywhere else I could pull off such a stunt.

"I want to work for myself, Lana. I'm too old to go backward and be some intern." I was thirty-four years old and had been out of the marketing game for the last five years. Having my own business on the side was hardly worth putting on my resume, and being a PA didn't exactly fit the bill. "I haven't worked properly in marketing for five years, and if I declare that I have my own company, that's going to look like a conflict of interest."

"Girl, sometimes I feel like you make up all manner of excuses to keep you with that man. I ain't never seen the type of relationship y'all have, and honestly, I don't think it's healthy."

God, I really didn't need this now. She was always taking some dig at Pat.

Yes, she had reasons to, like everyone else, because I

probably spent far too much time with him, but he wasn't the problem.

The problem was me.

"Why isn't it healthy?" I threw back. I knew full well what she meant, but I wanted to hear it.

"I think… I personally think being with him and sorting out his shit all the time is draining you. I think it's sucking up all the time you could be using to advance yourself. He calls you all the time, Georgie. Your job is supposed to finish at five, but damn, girl, he has you at his place until all hours of the night."

"We love playing games," I answered.

She shook her head at me and frowned. "This is my take: your relationship with the playboy is weird. He's codependent on you, and don't, for the love of God, tell me that 'we're just friends' bullshit. I know you like him on some level. How could you not? The man is gorgeous. I can't stand him, but I at least fess up that if he grabbed me for a round in bed, I wouldn't say no."

What the hell was she saying to me? "Lana, for God's sakes. First of all, it sounds more like a case of you liking him. Yes, he is gorgeous, but he's absolutely not my type."

"Girl, don't tell me you suddenly have a type. I've seen you with men of all different races. I've never seen him with a black woman, but that doesn't mean anything. I'm pretty certain he's into you and just waiting for the day when something happens between you two."

I frowned. "Oh Lord, Lana, that's not what I meant about type. I could never be with a man who is so... He's a womanizer. That's him. He's the poster boy for the playboys and should come with a warning label to keep far, far away. I know that, and to me, gorgeous as he is, that is the worst quality a man could have."

It was true, and that was where I'd stuck to my guns. Admittedly...

And I would only ever confess this to myself... In my moments of wishing I could be anyone else besides myself, I have on occasion wondered what it would be like to be on his arm and get all the attention he gave those airheaded women who fell at his feet and worshiped him. They did that, but he knew how to treat a woman. Just as long as she knew he wasn't for keeps.

I couldn't do that or be with a guy for fun.

"Okay, whatever you say. I wouldn't be a friend to you if I didn't point these things out. You need to think of it as a possibility though, Georgie. You can't deny that you spend a lot of time with him. Even if it's five minutes outside of your time, it's still time that you could have used to do something for yourself or do something for your dad."

My shoulders slumped. "I don't know what I'm

going to do. I need money big time to change things up. I can't continue to live like this."

I had a one-bedroom apartment that was just big enough to spin around in, and Dad lived in a similar sort of place.

That was the best we could get after his stroke.

I'd lived there with him after he came out of the hospital so I could look after him. That was a nightmare. I had no space to do anything. We'd lived like that for a year until I got the job at Flynns and was able to get my own little apartment, which was just down the road from his.

It was in East L.A., close enough to get to the city and just affordable enough to live in.

Neither place was ideal though, especially where Dad lived.

"Something will come up." Lana nodded.

Just then, my phone buzzed with a text message. I dug into my purse and retrieved it.

It was Pat.

He'd texted: **I need you. Can you come to me?**

Lana frowned and took the phone from me so she could get a read. She smiled to my surprise.

"How I wish that sounded more businesslike. It could be a booty call?" Mischief flickered in her eyes.

I chuckled and took the phone back from her. "Yes, that's what it is."

Better to just play along.

I texted back: **On my way.**

The blue dots started jumping almost immediately, and he said: **Thanks, baby.**

"Go, go with your boss friend. The two of you play whatever game it is you're playing. At least it's a distraction. Tomorrow, we'll brainstorm ideas."

I gave her another hug.

Brainstorm ideas. It felt like it was all I ever did.

Back to square one. Would I ever move from this square?

Would be nice to see what is was like on square two.

That building on Santa Monica Blvd had almost felt like mine.

I guess it was just a dream my heart wanted but could never have.

CHAPTER 5

Patterson

MOM GREETED me with a kiss on my cheek as I met her in the living room of our family home.

She'd been in there with one of the decorators, going over what she wanted to do for this year. She changed up the house every year.

She'd come over to me and gave me that kiss with a hug, then turned around to slip her arm around me to lead me toward the kitchen.

"Your dad's out back in the garden, eating lunch. Want something to eat? I made a veg casserole." Mom's eyes twinkled when she glanced at me over her shoulder.

"I'm good, Mom. I don't think I'm going to be here long enough to eat."

She frowned slightly, then did that thing where she was avoiding too much eye contact. It was a dead give-away that she and Dad had been talking, possibly argued, and he'd had his way.

My parents hardly argued, but I could always tell when they had.

In all instances, it was always best not to get involved.

On this occasion, I could almost guess what it was about, and I could guess too that Mom looked like she was on my side. It was the arm around me that suggested that. She'd always had a soft spot for me. Just not soft enough to go against Dad.

I'd been so upset yesterday that I couldn't even tell Georgie what was happening. She'd asked me several times what was wrong, but I thought it was better to keep it all to myself until I knew I'd done all I could to sweep Dad's crazy idea under the rug.

I'd kept all my anger in, saving it up for today. Lunchtime, like he said, and I was hoping like hell that he'd had time to think and would cut me some slack.

He sat out on the terrace, eating while he read a newspaper.

At least it was safe to say that the papers had nothing on me today.

Dad had the nerve to smile at me when he saw me. Mom released her arm and walked back into the house.

Another sign of defeat.

I pulled up a chair and sat in front of Dad.

He speared a mushroom with his fork and pointed it at me.

"Now, this is the perfect meal," Dad mused with a nod of satisfaction. "Cooked by the perfect woman who does everything perfectly. Even after fifty years, the food still tastes great and I always get her to make this casserole because she knows it's my favorite thing."

I just kept my eyes trained on him. I knew what he was trying to do and today, I was going to stand a little stronger in my decision.

"Dad. I've come to the conclusion that you've lost your mind," I told him, holding up my hands and flicking my palms over.

He laughed. "Okay, I may have lost my mind, but it's still my damn company, and you aren't getting jack unless you meet my specifications."

I gritted my teeth and frowned. A whole day and three hours later, and he was still singing from the same song sheet.

"Dad, what is the matter with you? Why do you want to hurt me?"

"Patterson, you think me wanting to see my only son with a good woman he's in love with means there's something wrong with me? You think that will hurt you?" He gave me a dubious look. "Really?"

"It's just so sudden. I don't get it. I know there was the stuff in the papers, but how could this be the only resolution you've come up with? Me getting married."

It was ridiculous, and I didn't understand why I wasn't being given any other options.

"Do you plan to get married someday, son, and have kids?"

I shook my head. "Nope."

"Why's that? Your mother and I have been great examples to you. Why wouldn't you want what we have?"

It wasn't that at all. "I'm not you guys. I know what I need in my life, and I don't think you have any right to do this to me. It's completely out of context, and you can't expect me to just sit there and take it."

He shrugged. "I think I can. Patterson, I've been too lenient with you over the years. This is why you are the way you are. In fact, I've always been like it. You were our IVF baby. Our one chance to have a child, a symbol of our love."

God, why?

Every minute I had to hear this story. In one context or another, whatever it was, Dad would make it fit. It wasn't even like they'd been that old when they had me. They had no age. Dad had been close to the age I was now, and Mom was thirty-five. It was just the fact that Mom was told she'd have difficulty having kids and they were married for ten years before they actually had me.

"Dad, again, I love and respect you. I get that I was your miracle baby, but damn, what does that have to do with me and the company?"

He leaned forward and smiled. "Boy, this is my one shot to get you to do something I know will be beneficial to you. It's the only chance I got to make you listen to me. You know I'm way serious, and I take it you want the business, or you wouldn't be here." He quirked a brow.

I bit the inside of my lip. This was like being a piece on a chessboard.

The king in checkmate by the king of the opposing side.

I might be in charge on some level, but I answered to a higher power, who could control me.

"You expect me to just go outside and pick up a woman you think is marriable?" That was me trying one last time.

"Here's the deal, Patterson. I don't have time to go around in circles with you. Since you're so great with meeting women, I doubt it will be a problem to get over the first hurdle. We live in L.A. Plenty of fish in the sea. Plenty of women I'm sure will be scrambling for your hand in marriage. You get engaged by the fundraiser, and I'll give you Miami Beach."

I straightened up, interest piquing.

Give me?

"What do you mean by 'give me,' exactly? Like it will actually be mine?" I eyed him curiously, wondering if he was serious.

"I will give it to you. It won't fall part of the company. It will be yours to call whatever you want. That's if you get engaged by the day of the fundraiser."

"*Six weeks?*"

He nodded. We hosted a charity fundraiser every year. We sponsored a different charity each time. This year it was the Multiple Sclerosis Society.

"Six weeks, Patterson. And I don't mean to just grab some old person off the road either. You need to invest time into finding this girl and treating her right. I need to believe you guys are in love. Then you have another two months until I actually retire. If you get married, then, and only then, will I sign over the whole empire to you."

Fuck, this was crazy.

But... he was offering me everything, and all I had to do was find a wife.

"Don't you think that's quick? What if it doesn't

work out? Can you really say you know somebody in that short space of time?"

"Fifty years of marriage, son? I met my girl two weeks prior to that, and it was enough time for me. If I can do that, you can too." He chuckled and popped the mushroom in his mouth.

Fucking hell, what was this?

But…how could I turn this down?

"I need a woman," I blurted as soon as Ivan sat down in my cozy chair.

My best buddy was not only married to the Queen of Hearts but the woman everyone called The Love Doctor.

He himself was a love doctor, and the two of them were the newly voted in hosts of the TV Show *The Love Doctor.*

Who better to get help from than Ivan and Jada St. James?

Well, just the Ivan part. I was pretty certain that Jada would laugh me to scorn.

Ivan burst out laughing. That wasn't what I needed, or what I expected. Not from him.

"I'm serious. Ivan, I need a woman. A wife."

He laughed even more. "Are you finally admitting you're on drugs?"

"I'm not on drugs." I quickly told him what was happening to me, and the smirk still remained on his face. "Ivan, can I ask why yu look like this is some joke to you?"

"Because it kind of is. I've never known you to have things clear cut and smooth. There's always one thing or another with you. Always." He was still laughing.

"You asshole, this is my life. Just imagine it. If Hudson takes over, that's my ass out the damn door. Fuck, he'll probably get Dad to take me with him as he leaves, like that old piece of furniture no one wants.'

"Oh my God, Patterson. This is crazy. What do you want me to say exactly?"

"I don't know. Man, you're a psychotherapist; this is the type of shit that can put a person in therapy. My old man wants me to grab a woman and marry her so I can inherit the family fortune. That's the kind of messed-up shit you see on *Jerry Springer*." I threw my hands up and widened my eyes.

Fuck, it was true. This was talk-show-worthy trash because it was just as ridiculous as the stories you saw on one of those shows. And I was the pawn, not the king. I was actually a pawn moving across the chessboard, not knowing what I was doing and waiting to get picked off by my cousin.

Six weeks to get engaged.

The thing was, I wanted Miami Beach. I wanted it badly.

Dad, that evil demon, he knew exactly how to rub me the right way and butter me up.

That project would be worth billions. I could have my very own thing, separate from the company, and believe me, I would indeed separate it.

How was I going to get there though?

"What about an ex-girlfriend who you connected with?" Ivan suggested. He said that as simply as if we were talking about passing jam and bread.

"Ivan, I can't believe how well you're taking this. Can't you at least look a little shocked by all this?"

He sat forward and rested his elbows on his knees. "Man, Jada and I were practically engaged after ten weeks. We got married three months later. Sure, we're newlyweds, but I know we're forever. If you want me to say it can't be done, then I'm not your guy. The only thing I have a problem with is that you had to be told to do this. It's different if it happens naturally. It's more real and special."

I rested my head back into the sofa.

I didn't know why I thought he'd be shocked because sure, he fell head over heels for Jada the minute he set his eyes on her. The thing, though, was all these examples of people falling for each other weren't like me.

"Ivan, I don't have the luxury of that. If I want the empire, I need to get in the mindset."

"Well, back to my question. What about ex-girl-friends? There was Phoebe. You said you saw her just the other day, right?"

"No, she's not wife material. She's annoying as fuck, and I wouldn't want to even introduce her to my parents."

Ivan narrowed his gaze at me. "Why'd you hook up with her, then?"

"Come on, man? Just because you're all loved up in your nest doesn't mean you have to forget how to be a guy. I just like sleeping with her."

"Okay, what about Sophie? You liked her too. You said she was a great cook. You have to get someone your dad will believe you're into. Your parents love to cook, so they can bond with someone like that."

I wish he didn't say all that, because it was irrelevant.

"No, not her either. She's just for the bedroom. One of my bed friends."

"Patterson, you know, I'm starting to see where your dad is coming from. *Bed friends*? Damn, man, I didn't know you were that bad. You are a fucking manwhore."

"Nah, man, do I look like some whore to you? Really?"

He rolled his eyes at me. "Okay, fine. What about Susan?"

"Fucking racist bitch." It was like I'd programmed my brain to say that every time her name was mentioned. She'd said something racist about Georgie, and that was it for me. I showed her the door.

"What the hell happened? She seemed so nice." He widened his eyes.

"No, Ivan, and I don't wish to go into that tonight. The whole thing made me feel like I didn't do enough to put her in her place, but that was just because if she were a guy, I would have decked her for what she said. She got away lightly for being a woman. Let's just leave it at that."

I had to focus and concentrate.

Ivan grit his teeth. "Patterson, maybe you should join a dating site. Then you could specify that you want a relationship worthy of marriage."

I looked at him like he'd just slapped me and spit in my tea. "That is the worst idea ever. Do you know what the hell kind of women I'll have after me? Oh my gosh. This is ridiculous as shit. I'm going to fucking lose everything I worked so damn hard for."

"Just calm down. Let's think. Think of someone

you'd want to marry. Pretend you went to the shop and picked her out. Like a new car. You love cars."

I loved cars. They weren't like women though. Not in the least.

"So, I go to the shop and pick her out. I may as well hire someone to …"

My voice trailed off as an idea formed in my mind.

Ivan frowned, seeing where my mind was going.

"Patterson, you can't just hire someone to marry you. Your dad will know. Trust me."

I shook my head. I was a desperate man willing to do anything at this point.

"We can practice, he'd never know."

"Now that is crazy. You can't fake all that."

"Well, maybe it could be someone I have been with."

"Patterson, I may have mentioned a few girls I knew of, but we both know at the end of the day, those bitches would run to the press with the story the first chance they got. They would, trust me. Same as a person who you hired could."

"I'll pay them well. What's a few hundred thousand to a multi-billion-dollar fortune?"

Ivan shook his head. "I'm not supporting this. Not one damn bit. Here's my last piece of advice, then I'm going. You need to calm down and think. You need to find a woman who you trust. That's the first thing, the first step and a hurdle in any relationship. Trust. Someone you trust, someone who trusts you. Then you move to the next part where you feel you'll do anything for her, and she'll do anything for you. Then you can't live without each other."

My attention was drawn to the front door opening.

Georgie was coming through it with a bag of groceries. She smiled when she saw the two of us.

"Hey, guys." Her smile widened. "I hope you guys are hungry. I'm making enchiladas."

Georgie...

Yasssss.

Ivan was my best friend, but there was no one on this earth I trusted more than this woman. I trusted her, and she trusted me. She trusted me enough to sleep in the same bed as me and know I wouldn't try anything with her.

There wasn't a damn thing I wouldn't do for her, and she'd shown me time after time that she would do anything for me.

While I was sure she could live perfectly without me, I knew I couldn't live without my wonderful PA.

How far would she be willing to go for me?

I looked back to Ivan. He was shaking his head at me and mouthing *no.*

I smiled, ignoring him, and nodded.

Georgie...She was perfect.

CHAPTER 6

Georgie

As I LISTENED to Pat speak, I was reminded of a sermon Dad's pastor gave one Sunday when I was nine years old.

It was something about kindness and loving thy neighbor. Being the good Samaritan. The story stuck in my mind and stayed there because I always wondered what I'd be willing to do for a person.

Listening to Pat now, I wondered the same.

Many thoughts flew through my mind as he proposed his new craziness to me. *Many,* many thoughts.

None of them good, and I had to apologize sincerely to God because today, I didn't think I could be anything that resembled the Good Samaritan.

We sat around the kitchen counter. The frying pan was close.

If hitting him with it would knock some sense into him, I might try that. But that could get me fired, which would be very bad.

The jug of juice I'd made was also close by, so I could have tossed that in his face, but I figured there was a chance doing that could get me fired too.

He stopped talking, and I was looking at him, looking at him but not really seeing him.

Looking at him and more like thinking about what he was asking me to do.

Be his wife...

His fake wife...

Fake fiancée first though. Oh no, no, I couldn't forget that part, and he'd planned it all out. What we could do, and how we'd fool old man Richard into handing over his empire. Basically showing him who's boss.

Basically...

That was how he'd phrased it, as if there was anything basic in all of this.

How had my life come to this point?

How?

I pulled in a deep breath and closed my eyes tight, squeezing them shut.

I could answer my own damn question perfectly and in fact with ease.

How did *I* come to this point? The answer was me.

I allowed this. I allowed my life to become more shit than it had already been, and Lana was a hundred percent correct. I needed to leave. I needed to leave Pat and divert my life back to where it once was.

I was at the stage in my life where there was a calm after the storm. The tornado had blown through, and like Dorothy in *The Wizard of Oz*, it sent me to some strange land, and now I had to find my way back. The only difference between Dorothy and me was that I was sent to a strange man, and instead of finding my way home, I had to find the way back to myself.

"Georgie, say something," Pat said, shaking my hand.

I opened my eyes and glared at him. First, I stared right at him, and then down at our hands, where he'd rested his on the top of my knuckles.

How I could have wished that at this point in my life that I'd be engaged to someone who actually loved me.

Fuck...

In my bucket list, I'd penned me down as married by twenty-eight, living in the suburbs with our two kids.

We'd live in a house that my imaginary husband would have bought for us because of the unique style, and he'd be a man of integrity and honor.

My husband was supposed to be a man who, when I looked at him, I'd feel like he was my life's accomplishment.

Not this guy in front of me, who went through women like he breathed air. I couldn't even use the usual random phrases, like he went through women like he changed clothes, because for him, it was faster than that. He could wake up tomorrow, meet one woman for breakfast, sleep with her, get to work, meet another woman for lunch, sleep with her, get back to work, meet another woman or two for dinner and sleep with them.

Jesus... Why was I still sitting here?

I pulled my hands from his and stood up on shaky legs.

I couldn't talk, not just yet. My brain was still processing stuff. If I left now, as in left him and my job, I'd have two months of savings to live off.

It would kind of be like when Dad first got sick but worse because back then, I had savings that took care of us for a year.

"Georgie..." He held my gaze, and I saw red flashes of light flickering all around me.

Maybe this was how a bull felt in the ring. My hand took on a life of its own and reached for the closest thing. It happened to be my glass of orange juice.

I grabbed it and threw the drink straight in his face, then I set the flute-shaped glass back down on the granite worktop.

Shock registered all over his face, but he surprised me by coming after me when I stormed away from him.

He grabbed my arm.

Big mistake. It was a big mistake to come after me in the first place because when I got like this, the only result was what I did next.

The same hand that had thrown the drink in his face landed a slap right across his cheek when I whirled around to face him. I slapped him so hard it left an instant mark.

He released me, now looking stunned.

"How dare you? How very dare you?" I cried, my voice shaking.

"Georgie, what the hell? You just slapped me."

"Yes, you asshole. Newsflash, you had it coming."

His shoulders slumped. "Georgie, I'm desperate."

"Desperate. If you're that desperate, go do exactly as your father says. Find a woman, not me. I may be of the sex, but I will never be associated with those bitch whores you gather in your fold. You forget I know you,

Patterson Flynn. I know everything about you, and you want me to tarnish the one thing a girl should dream about just because you want to get your family fortune." I couldn't stop my voice from shaking.

I couldn't stop shaking.

"We'd pretend, Georgie. People have failed marriages all the time. People get married, and then one of them leaves or does something to the other and the marriage breaks down."

That... what he just said was a perfect example of how selfish he was. It was all about him. So much so that he didn't even realize what he just said. The same way I knew him, he knew me too. He knew I was a child of a seriously bad relationship, and the disastrous marriage my parents had.

"If I mattered to you at all, you'd know that I'm well versed in witnessing a failed marriage and I don't want that for myself. I lived through it in the worst way."

It was only when I said that, that he realized what he'd said. "Georgie, I'm sorry. I wasn't thinking."

Mom had left our family, but it was after she'd made her mark. She was always cheating on Dad, and he knew about it. Dad was a fireman and always at work. She used the opportunity to sneak men into the house. Not just any old guys either. Drug dealers and men who didn't care about how young you were. The year before she left, one of the men grabbed me, ready to rape me. It must have been God who saved me that day because Dad came home just at that time and beat the guy to a pulp. I was only eleven years old.

That was the day when I saw a very ugly side of the world, but it opened my eyes to how bad a relationship could be. Better to be alone than with someone who could hurt you the way Mom had hurt all of us. Angelica had followed in her footsteps, and I hadn't seen either one of them in years. Mom, I didn't expect to see ever again. Angelica, well...

It looked like she would follow that path again.

I shook my head at him. "I'm not doing this for you. I won't tarnish my name with this hanging over my head. Imagine if we get engaged and everyone will know. It will be all over the place. Then we get married and divorced in six months. That's practically three quarters of a year of my life with you, pretending."

"Exactly. Pretending. Georgie, I know it's fucking farfetched. I know it's the craziest thing I've ever asked you to do, but I don't have anyone else to ask. I can't do it the normal way either because any good woman with sense realistically wouldn't choose me."

I couldn't disagree with him.

Patterson Flynn might look like God took his own sweet time to make him the masterpiece of a man he was, but he was what you called pretty packaging with destruction inside. Pandora's box. I was certain the box was nice; open the box, and demons and evil would fly out.

That was him.

"Pat, I don't know what to say to you. My life can't go down this path with you. People already give me slack for being one of your bed friends, and I take it. Most men won't even date me because they know I'm always with you. And I mean the good guys. I just haven't addressed that shit yet because I have too much going on."

He held my gaze, looking at me with the desperation he spoke of. "You're my best friend. Forget work, forget everything. This is us... you and me. Georgie, you're my best friend. I've known Ivan my whole life, and we used to get up to some crazy shit together. But that's just it. This is different. So different I could only ask someone who I really trust. I have no plans to get married, Georgie, and if I did for real, the kind of person my Dad is talking about for me to find would never pick me. But... that's my fault. So, this is the only thing I can think of doing in the time scale he's given me, and you are the only person I know who'd have my back. It's a lot to ask, but I'm not just asking you to do it for nothing." He gave me a tentative expression. "I hope I don't insult you further by offering you a million dollars to do this. To be my fake fiancée. I'll give you a million dollars upfront if I get the Miami Beach project. And I'll give you another million after my father signs everything over to me. I can't lose my legacy over this crazy demand of his. That isn't fair. I can't lose it, and I can't lose it to someone like my asshole of a cousin. So, that's it. That is how serious I am about this."

I stared at him, and now I was reminded of the conversation I had with Lana yesterday. When I repeated what she'd always told me about closed doors.

The door was closed on me with Marsha's campaign because I wasn't supposed to go through that door.

Just now, another door opened for me.

Two million dollars.

Two.. million dollars...

Jesus... How could I say no to that?

Two million dollars in total.

I could do everything I wanted with just the first million. Buy Dad a house and set up my business properly. Hell, I wouldn't even need a loan or a mortgage.

But... doing this...

It was like selling my soul. I'd always imagined my knight in shining armor asking me to marry him. Getting a ring and proposing to me properly. Just like in the movies.

Just like that, and I'd cry just like that because I was so in love that I couldn't believe it was happening.

Again, it was a dream my heart wanted.

The door had opened, but would I be going through it?

"I need time. I need..." I turned and walked away from him, walking out.

CHAPTER 7

Georgie

I CALLED Lana and told her everything.

I felt that she would give me some grounds to be objective and make the decision based on that instead of desperation.

However, my best friend shocked me to the core when she told me to accept.

She told me to accept the offer.

She pointed out that it would be a total of nine months of my life that I'd have to sacrifice, and she also sneakily pointed out that I was already acting like his wife. She couldn't think of any difference in how the situation would be. Talk about major shade.

I was listening though. She made some good points, and I knew it was shock that had taken me.

There was however one other person I had to speak to.

Dad was always objective. No matter what. He always gave people the benefit of the doubt. He also always had the ability to weigh a situation and assess the good and the bad in it.

That was what I needed now.

I was completely blown away in the worst way possible by the situation, but there was a light at the end of the tunnel I wanted to be certain was the right light to aim for.

Good as it was, I was thinking long term.

Unlike Pat, I did plan for marriage and kids. When that happened, how could I lie to my future husband and tell him first of all that I got married to my boss, and it simply didn't work out? It would be a lie, and then I'd have to live with the fact that I was paid two million dollars to sign my name and life away.

The lies really got to me. I was hoping talking to Dad would give me some clarity one way or the other.

I went to see Dad once or twice a day. He was able to cook and move around the house, but I wanted to make sure he had everything he needed.

Today's visit was earlier than normal. I went to see him first thing in the morning. Usually, I'd go just before lunch and then after work. Sometimes we'd have dinner together. On Sunday, that was a definite because we'd always done that when I was a kid.

As I turned on the corridor leading to his apartment, Dr. Thompson was leaving. My heart sped up at the sight of him because as far as I knew, he only visited Dad once a month, and he'd already been here this month. He was part of Dad's community care team. When Dad first had the stroke and couldn't move, the team was here every day.

"Dr. Thompson." I couldn't keep the panic out of my voice.

I made the poor man jump because of the pace at which I'd rushed up to him.

"Miss French. It's good to see you." Dr. Thompson nodded. He was the same age as Dad and had that fatherly warmth about him.

"You too. Is my dad okay?"

He sighed and adjusted the thick bone-rimmed glasses on his face. "I was going to call you later. After this evaluation. Your father called last night complaining of chest pains. We sent an ambulance to him, and they thought he was okay enough to stay at home."

I gasped. "What? He didn't call me. He didn't tell me

69

anything." He also never said anything after I stopped by with food. That was just before I went to Pat.

"It was really late last night, and he's... concerned about involving you any more than he already has. You're his next of kin and have signed power of attorney from him, so I'm obliged to tell you, but realistically, he doesn't want you doing more for him, or him being a burden, as he said."

"I will do anything for him." I nodded.

"I know, and many wish they could have a daughter like you."

"Thank you, I appreciate it. What's happening, Dr. Thompson?" I brought my hands together to stop them from shaking.

The shadow in his expression displaying a wealth of worry made me feel worse.

"His heart is getting bad. The valves aren't working like they should. We've been trying all these years to fix the problem that first resulted in the stroke, and it looks like he could have another one. I don't want that, but the alternative is expensive. He needs surgery. Plus, the apartment isn't really set up for a sick person. He's finding it difficult to move around, and that's placing extra pressure on his heart. He said the elevator wasn't working the other day, so he ended up climbing the stairs for five flights. I'm impressed he didn't end up in the hospital after that."

My own heart squeezed on hearing that. Dad never told me he had to do that, and the last thing I wanted was for him to feel like a burden on me.

He was all I had, my everything.

Atrial fibrillation was what he'd had. That was what caused the stroke. I read about it, researched it, and made sure I knew everything so I could help him in whatever way he needed.

It was what happened when the chambers of the heart didn't work as they should. That came from faulty electrical signaling. For him, it was due to having heart valve disease. He hadn't even known he had it until that time.

I wasn't surprised Dad had problems with his heart because of the hell he'd been through with Mom and Angelica.

"What do I need to do?" I asked.

"We need to talk about surgery. I'm just going to be straight up real with you. That is the best way forward, and his insurance won't cover the procedure I'm talking about. So, we need to talk costs of care, his after care and in-patient care too. Should the surgery be successful, he'll most likely be in the hospital for six to eight weeks so we can monitor him. Then... realistically, my next recommendation would be that he moves from here. If you can't arrange that, then he'd probably need to go to a care home. This place isn't appropriate for him anymore, and it definitely won't work after surgery."

Lord...

It was too much, and I was selfish. I was being offered two million to be my boss' fake fiancée and questioning it.

Me being me, wanting to hold on to some dignity. What was dignity and a dream if my father was desperate?

"Thank you."

"No worries. I'll call you, and we can make an appointment to talk properly when I have figures and a plan. Then you'll have something to work with."

I nodded.

In that fatherly way, he gave me one last smile before leaving.

I went in and saw Dad. He was standing by the window, resting his right arm on his walking stick. It had taken him two years before he was able to walk again.

His speech was never affected the way most peoples were after a stroke. It was his body. The whole right side was immobilized, and he could barely move his left leg.

He turned and saw me, offered up a smile, which fell when he saw how worried I looked.

"I just saw Dr. Thompson," I began and walked over to him.

"I guess he told you what happened," Dad sighed.

"Yes, Dad. Please, don't ever feel like you can't call me. I love you."

His eyes glistened with tears. "I love you too, and I never wanted to be this burden on you at this stage in your life. I'm sorry, sweet girl."

"No Dad, don't you ever apologize to me or think you're a burden. I'll fix it. I'll take care of everything. Just don't worry. Please."

"It's too much, baby girl. Too much on you, too much on me. I know you'd sell your soul if you could, and I'd have to spend eternity trying to get it back."

"No, trust me. I'll sort it all out. Pat gave me an offer I can't refuse."

There it was, my decision.

The door was open, and I was going through it.

I didn't see Pat when I went into work the next day.

He didn't message me to say he'd be late or anything, so I knew he'd be at home. I also knew his lack of messages was his way of giving me space to think.

I went straight to his house after lunch.

There he was, sitting on the sofa, playing *Call of Duty*.

I thought of the first time we spoke about our love for games.

When Mom first left, Dad had to leave me and Angelica with our neighbors while he worked.

It was then I made my first close friendship with a guy I wasn't into. Rory Tanner was obsessed with video games, and he dragged me into his addiction.

We played every day after school, and every summer saw us indoors, playing some battle.

It was my escape. I still spoke to him and every once in a while I'd get a text when a new game came out, asking me what I'd thought about it.

Patterson was my adult version of Rory. My guy best friend, who just happened to be my boss asking me to be his fake fiancée.

He glanced over at me. His piercing green eyes bore into me with the desperation from last night.

He was shirtless, muscles and tattoos on full display. He dropped the handset next to him and stood up. With his sweatpants hanging low on his hips, the perfect V-cut shape of his torso was visible. He looked like an ad for *Men's Health* or some fitness magazine.

I just hoped like hell no one was in his bedroom and he was alone.

"Is anyone else here?" I asked, looking around.

The worst incident was when I'd come here and saw him in bed with two women.

God, this really did feel like selling my soul.

"No, it's just me."

I gave him a long and hard stare. It almost bordered on cold. The kind you would give the devil if he wanted something from you.

"I've thought long and hard, and I will accept, but there have to be certain things... I want certain things." I didn't know what I expected, but he didn't look as happy as I thought he'd be.

"What are they?" he asked. That surprised me too because he jumped straight to that.

"No whores... I mean it, Patterson. No whores. If I have to go along with this pretense, you have to pretend too. I want respect, so you can't have any side women, bed friends, strippers, just no shit like that. No whores, Pat." I didn't realize how much that all bothered me until now. "If you're with me, then you're with me, and that's what I want people to see. Nothing that would embarrass me. I want, when I lie to my actual husband in the future, that it at least looks like we had a legit relationship. Like I actually fell for you. And not like you paid me."

God, that was what it was.

If it was just the whole aspect about my business, I could have cried it off and did as Lana suggested by figuring out other ideas.

Shit got real when it came to Dad. I wasn't going to play around with his life. I would never forgive myself if something happened to him and I knew there was something I could have done to save him.

Pat walked up to me and looked me over. "Done. No whores."

"I mean it, Pat. I know what you're like, and I loathe that about you. I absolutely loathe it. It's vile, and I wish you weren't like that. So, if you want me to do this, you tell me now if you can promise me there will be no other women, and you act like you love me."

He reached out and touched my face. The warmth of his hands seeped into my skin and scattered my nerves.

"I do love you."

"That's not what I mean. You know what I mean, Pat. I'm talking about real love. You're very manipulative, so it shouldn't be that hard for you."

He looked hurt when I said that and pulled his hand away. I knew saying that was a little below the belt, but he couldn't exactly refute it because it was true.

"Georgie, I thank you for doing this for me, and I promise you on my life and all I have at stake, you'll be the only woman in my life for the time we're together."

A tear ran down my cheek, and I wiped it away quickly.

"Okay, it's done. I'll do it. Pat... if you let me down in any way, I'll never forgive you."

He shook his head at me. "Baby, I may be the devil, and this person here who would never deserve you even if he were paid the whole Flynn empire, but you know I'd never let you down. That's why you use it against me. You're my weakness for some damn reason. So, please, just trust me. I won't let you down."

We stared at each other for a few seconds. I was too worked up to think about the sweetness in what he said. Between this craziness and what happened this morning, I was already drained.

"What's going on with you, Georgie? Everything aside, what's up?" He narrowed his gaze on me and looked at me like he was searching my soul.

"Nothing," I lied. He knew about Dad, knew I took care of him, and that was all. There was that line I drew again between us.

When he asked how he was, I told him he was doing okay. I never allowed him to ever see how worried I was, and I'd never allow him to see how freaked out I was now about Dad's health and all that he needed.

I always felt and lived by the code that sometimes, it was best not to show a person how desperate you were. Especially a person who had power over you.

Again, it showed weakness. It showed them you needed them.

"Something's up with you. You don't normally say what you're thinking. Definitely not to me." He assessed.

"Maybe I should give you a piece of my mind more often."

"Maybe you should."

"You drive me crazy, Pat."

He smiled. "You can be crazy all you want frolicking on Miami Beach with your millions. Imagine it, baby. You and me standing on the balcony of one of the apartments, looking at our fortune." He nodded.

I gave him a weak smile. "Yeah. That sounds great."

"Can I hug you? Not a victory hug. It's more the sort where I know there's something up with you and you're not saying, and I just want to give you a hug because it will help in my own small way."

Only he could say nonsense like that and make me smile when I felt like this.

I smiled and fell into his embrace, resting my head on the hard walls of his chest as he circled his arms around me.

At least as I did that, I did feel some comfort.

There was nothing to feel bad about and wouldn't be if it all went to plan. I just had to pretend, and it would all be fine.

Pretend...

I'd have it all. Dad would get taken care of, get his

new house, and I'd get the startup capital for my business.

It was all and more.

I just wished I didn't have a bad feeling about this.

CHAPTER 8

Patterson

I WATCHED HER.

Georgie grabbed her notebook and sat on the love seat.

She had her hair down today and draped it to the side in that habitual way I always thought was sexy.

She would probably kill me if she knew I thought that.

Last night was intense.

I should have felt happier than this considering she'd agreed to this crazy plan of mine.

I should have been ecstatic that I'd actually gotten

one up on Dad, but no, I did not feel like that because this was wrong.

In my crazy mind when I put the idea to Georgie, I didn't expect her to react the way she did.

Truth be told, I was ashamed to admit that I expected her to be on board with it just like she was with everything else. I say 'Jump,' and she asks how high.

She was the last person I wanted to treat that way.

It showed how much of a selfish bastard I was to not have contemplated that she might hold things like marriage close to her heart, and I was this loathsome creature who would essentially spoil that dream for her.

In my head, we'd get together, get married, and get divorced. Bim bam boom. Done.

In her head, it was a failure she'd have to declare to the person she was meant to be with when the time came.

Everything she'd said last night cut me deep. It expressed what she thought of me, and I knew in my heart that I had no business asking her to do something like this.

The thing was... it was believable. Me and her.

It was actually believable, and that was what made this plan so good.

I couldn't count the number of times my parents

had asked me about us and I insisted that we were seriously just friends.

Ivan too brought it up once and once only. It didn't escape me that he'd just mentioned it the one time in the time I'd known her. I didn't know why that was when everyone else had taken a dig at me every chance they got.

Dad would believe it. Mom would believe it. The only actual people who would know the truth were Georgie and me. Ivan too.

He'd know the truth. He'd looked at me and saw that plan formulate in my mind and shocked me by shaking his head in disapproval.

When she came in, I'd thought it was weird how neither of us had mentioned her in the mix. She was perfect.

I planned to tell Dad that in my search, I never saw what was right in front of me. Then all we'd have to do was be ourselves. That part wasn't hard. This was like adding gravy to a fine meal. We got it easy, got off easy, and we'd be filthy rich for it.

She deserved more than this. More than me, but I was hoping having all that money would make up for any bad feelings she felt toward the plan and what we'd have to do.

What I didn't expect though was to feel this way.

Hearing she thought all that negative stuff about me made me stop and want to take a look at myself.

It made me stop and take a look at the looming question that floated through the air.

She'd agreed to do this for the money. Of course that was the most enticing part of this plan for her. Like anyone else she clearly agreed to do it for the money. But... and there was a massive big but in the way and it was down to what I'd noticed.

Georgie agreed not because she wanted the money, but it felt more to me like she needed it. Needed, not wanted.

A person who wanted the money would have agreed the night before, right off the bat when I first put the proposal to her. If I knew money would have enticed her, I would have gone in straight away with that.

A woman like her, however, didn't value or lust after money the way a majority of people did.

It was why she said she had to think about it.

I didn't know anyone in this hemisphere who got offered two million and said they needed to think about it.

Sure, it was life-changing money, but it seemed to me like she would have turned my ass down if she didn't want that money for something.

I assumed it would be to buy a house, or do something for her father.

I wouldn't ask though. It was that line of privacy again. A line I wouldn't cross. She was doing enough for me.

She lifted her head and got her pen ready to write after scanning through her phone.

"We need a time frame and dates," she said.

"Where do you want to go, baby?" I knew she meant dates as in date, like the day in the month, but I was trying to be silly and bring some lightheartedness back to us. We weren't these serious people here talking business at my place.

She laughed. "Pat, not dates like that. But, while you mention it, I do need to sort myself out for an actual date."

"What? You don't have to do anything. You're perfect."

"Yes, of course, says the guy who will only go out with a girl who's modelled for Chanel or Victoria's Secret, oh, and *Sports Illustrated*. Mustn't forget that."

I went to protest but stopped myself. She was right.

"Georgie, you are just as beautiful, if not more beautiful than any of those women. Please don't change yourself."

"Great. Perfect. I almost believed you." She smiled and gave me a little clap.

My lips parted. I was being serious. "You should believe me because it's true."

"Okay, Pat, let's not overdo it. Anyway, this all needs to be believable. We need to have a time frame on when to do certain things. Including the said date. We need to do stuff to cause a stir in the public's eye."

I laughed. "You don't mean the stir like what was in the papers the other day?"

She shook her head vigorously. "No, sir, I do not mean that. Oh my gosh, I can't believe you even did that in public." She gave me that distasteful look that made me want to check what I said again.

I'd have to now. Seeing her as one of the guys was a thing of the past. It became so when I agreed to only be with her throughout this whole thing.

I'd promised her, and I absolutely was going to stand by that promise.

"Won't happen again."

She quirked a brow. "We'll see about that."

"So, what do you want us to do? I think we should do more together at the office, then go on a date somewhere everyone knows me."

She nodded. "Yes, I was thinking the Shangri La. That would be perfect. I'm always booking reservations for you there."

Because I knew that was the classiest place I could show off to a woman.

"Is that where you want to go?"

"No, not really. I kind of don't want to be a number, but if it works, then it works."

"No, it doesn't work." If we were going out, I at least wanted to take her somewhere she'd enjoy. "Where do you want to go? Name the place, and we'll go."

"Really?" She straightened, and her hair swished over her shoulders.

I sat forward. "Yes. Anywhere."

"Even if it's not your kind of place?" She eyed me curiously and got me curious too. It sounded like she had somewhere in mind.

Where was she thinking of going? Other than our crazy obsession with video games, we didn't really go out, or hang out like that. Then again, we were always doing work-related things.

"Of course."

"Well, I guess as long as it's a place where people will see you and know you, it should work, right?"

"Yeah. So, don't keep me in suspense. Where is it?" Maybe the question I should have asked was 'What is it?' because she suddenly got a wary look on her face.

"Okay… so, it has to do with jazz."

"Oh God." I winced and frowned. That was me coming out now. I couldn't help it. She knew a lot about me but probably not how I felt about jazz.

Grandfather always had it playing in his house. He

lived through a time when it was the in thing. He fought in WW2 as a pilot in the Air Force.

He might take the record for the person to get married the most in the family, but he was with my grandmother for the longest, before she died. They met back then, and all they talked about was jazz and the great swing bands of that time.

"Pat, you asked me, and I'm telling you," Georgie bubbled.

"What is this thing, Georgie?"

"1940s Night at The Globe next Friday." She lifted her shoulders, and her face brightened, like the thought was the best thing in the world.

"Oh my God, Georgie, what does this 1940s Night involve?"

She giggled and set her notebook down. "It's exactly as it sounds. You get dressed up and go right back to a time when it was cool. The fifties and sixties were cool too, but I should have lived during the forties."

"Baby, even with the war?" I bit the inside of my lip.

"That was the point of the music. It brought people together and took their minds away from what was happening. And the clothes were just to die for. I want to go dressed in some chic gown with my hair period styled and everything."

"It sounds like something Grandfather would go to.

Pretty certain his spirit will be there, ogling all the young women like you. The old ones too."

The smile fell from her face, and she glowered at me. "You are such an ass, you know that? Why get my hopes up, then drop me flat?"

"I thought you were going to say something cooler, like the Bread Bin." That was a seriously trendy club that opened last year.

"Oh, sure, let's go to a place where all your bed bunnies hang out." She grabbed her notebook.

"Bed bunnies?" I raised my brows.

"Pat, you know what I mean. I don't want to go somewhere where your women will be looking at me and judging me, and comparing me."

"You're beautiful. What the fuck do they have to compare?"

She leaned forward and narrowed her eyes at me. "*You...*" She pointed at me and shook her head. "You are an absolute man-bitch. You tell me that, but I'm not the kind of woman you'd be with. It's fine to have me around the place, running my fingers into the ground cooking, cleaning, doing all manner of shit for you. Basically, *The Help.* But if you saw me in somewhere like the damn Bread Bin, you'd look right over my head. Actually, you wouldn't even see me. Your evil little green eyes are programmed to find the easiest lay that suits your liking."

Oh my God…

How did we start talking about this?

And… man-bitch?

"First of all, you are not the damn help. Jesus, Georgie, if you felt like you were working too hard, all you had to do was put me in my place if I stepped out of line. Next, *evil little green eyes?* You make me sound like a leprechaun."

"You wish. They bring people luck. You make people crazy. There's a big difference."

I stared at her. She stared me down with that crude assumptive expression on her pretty face.

"So, this is exactly what being married to you is going to be like?" I mused

"Don't joke about that. You will get ten percent of the married version of me."

I couldn't help but laugh. "Ten percent? What would ninety percent be like?"

"You don't get to know." She sat back in the chair and huffed.

"Come on, tell me. You don't tell me that stuff. I'm curious." I was.

Mischief flickered in her eyes. "Ninety percent of me would be damn sexy, we wouldn't leave the bedroom, and my husband wouldn't be able to take his hands, or eyes, off me."

I'd known this woman for just over five years. In

that whole time, she'd said some outlandish things to me. Never like that though. And I'd never felt the yearning in the pit of my stomach like I just did. Thinking of a damn sexy version of her actually made my mouth water, like I was hungry and waiting on a fine meal.

I had to blink to refocus. "What's ten percent, then?" I had to ask.

"It's five percent of what you get now." A wicked smile lifted the corners of her pretty mouth.

"Five percent? Jesus, why is it less?"

"It just is."

"What if we go to this thing at The Globe. Can I at least get fifteen percent? Like during this time."

She laughed. "Seven and a half."

"You are one tough cookie, Miss Lady."

"Yes, well, savor the cookie, mister. You will not be with anyone else like me, because there is no one else like me, and you're damn lucky I agreed to marry your ass."

Now was the part where I could have said she was getting paid, but I knew deep down that really bothered her. The thing was, realistically, she was priceless to me as a PA. I knew her words as truth because I wouldn't have been able to find anyone else like her, or better than her.

It was the same thing here.

Curiosity filled me though. I was curious to see this play out. I benefitted from this little plan of ours a hundred percent more than her, but I was curious to get to see even more than seven and a half percent of the *damn sexy version* of her.

"I want twelve percent at The Globe. In public, I need that." I couldn't believe I was agreeing to go. "You want me to focus on you more than I already do, give me more."

She rolled her eyes at me and smiled. "Okay... you get twelve percent. Kudos to me for getting you to agree to The Globe. You do realize that it's more believable to be seen there with me than anywhere else."

That was true. On a real date I would have gone somewhere she'd like, or somewhere we'd both like.

"Okay, you win, and kudos to you for getting me to agree to go." At least The Globe had some association with two of the country clubs Dad went to. It sounded like the sort of event where we'd get a mixture of people and age groups. I was sure there'd be people there who would definitely recognize me. People in Dad's circles.

"I think if we create a buzz first with some public appearances and then get people talking, that should put the ball in motion."

Nothing spreads fire faster than the public, and a

buzz was what we needed. I'd pick the place next time though. I'd take her to a club.

"What else would you like me to do?" she asked.

"I thought we'd go at your pace." I wanted to be sure she was comfortable with everything.

In my head, I saw us making a show of this relationship in a way that would be so obvious that something was up. Like grabbing her and kissing her right in front of Dad. Then announcing our engagement. That would have been the complete wrong thing to do. Especially the kissing part.

I'd thought about that last night. I didn't know how she'd feel about that, but nothing would say we were together more than a kiss. A kiss in public.

"Let's start with being seen more around the office. I'll be sure not to slap you and be more loving toward you in public. I also won't throw anything at you. Then we get to Friday and see what happens after that. We could do different things every other day or just play it by ear. Then, maybe we could be set to get engaged either the same week as the fundraiser or at the fundraiser."

Good plan. Scary though, as that would be the first milestone.

"Thank you... Thank you again for agreeing to do this for me." Jokes aside along with curiosity. Again, I knew I was set to benefit from this a hundred percent more than her.

"You're welcome. I guess I can't complain or even make my demands. Two million is a lot of money, Pat. I can't believe you'd be willing to pay me that."

It was actually a small drop in the well. "You know the wealth in the business, Georgie. It's nothing."

"Well, if I get it, it will do life-changing things for me."

I was tempted again to ask her what she'd do, but I held back and decided to be subtle. "Hey, don't change on me too much and leave me."

"Do you think I'll still need to work for you if I get all that money?" She laughed.

That never crossed my mind. "I need you, baby. You can't leave me flat on my face with the twelve percent of you in my head."

She chuckled. "Let's cross that bridge when we get there." The humor left her eyes, and she looked more serious. "Does Ivan know?"

"He knew I was going to ask you, but he doesn't know the outcome." I hadn't spoken to him about that part yet. I would later. "Did you speak to Lana?"

She spoke to Lana about everything. I was certain she would have told her.

She nodded. "Yeah, is that okay? I just needed to talk to someone else about it."

There again was evidence of her considering the proposal. "Yeah, of course. What did she say?"

"You know Lana. It's two million."

Lana would have been the example of someone agreeing to the money straight away. "Yet you had to think about it?"

"It's different for me. I actually want to get married someday, and I don't want to get divorced. But hey, I'll cross that bridge too when we get there." The smile returned to her face, and she seemed to push her concerns away.

It didn't mean that I did though. I knew it was different for her, and I was going to make damn certain I'd make it up to her.

CHAPTER 9

Georgie

"How are you feeling?" Lana asked.

She set the tray down with our cookies and sat opposite me in the wicker chair.

We were sitting out on my little balcony, probably the best part of my teeny apartment.

It had a great view of the city and the Woodland area. For me, it was a view that gave me the best of both worlds.

How was I feeling though?

Not sure. I was trying, so maybe that was the best answer.

"Does doing my best count as an answer?"

"No." She laughed and started munching on a chocolate chip cookie. "Not for someone who's about to be a millionaire. Girl, if I were you, I'd be celebrating. I don't know what the big deal is. I don't even see what the deal is anyway. There's no problem. I'd do it before my heart could take another beat. Plus, it's not like Pat is some kind of toad. Wasn't he named the sexist man alive the other year?"

Yes, Pat was named that by FHM. He had so many titles like that, I lost track.

As his PA, I didn't just manage his office schedule; I managed his public appearances too. Fundraisers and charity events he was always being summoned to, and then were the magazine appearances. Who knew the life of a property developer would be that involved?

I broke up with Ty because I didn't like the whole public eye thing; now I was signing up for it.

Lana was right though. There was no big deal, and I was acting silly by not basking in the fact that I was a few weeks away from being a millionaire.

"I should be happier."

"Why aren't you?" She looked me over.

"Part of me wonders if this is it. I know, it's silly, and it's not like I'm being required to sell my virginity or something. It's just that getting engaged was the last thing I had left that was special to me. Part of my dreams. This isn't real, and that part gets to me. That's all it is. Plus, I don't exactly want that whole thing about being judged by the host of women he's been with."

Lana smiled. "Honey, who cares about what they think? He didn't ask them; he asked you, and honey, you should see that as a plus and take advantage of it." She nodded excitedly.

I laughed. "Take advantage? Maybe when it all sinks in and I can think more about the money, I'll be more excited about it."

"I get what you're saying, but I can't see why you're not thinking of that part nowwwwww. Georgie, think of the bigger picture. A place for your dad, and not just any old place. You can get him anything he wants. Think of how he'll feel, Georgie. I know he went through so much too."

Hearing her say that warmed my heart, and I nodded. The backs of my eyes stung when I thought of how horrible the last six years had been. The first year was perhaps the worst in my life. Even in comparison to my horrible childhood mishaps with Mom. That first year was extremely bad. It was the absolute nightmare I'd feared because Dad was my rock and suddenly, he was in this vulnerable state where I had to take care of him.

He'd only been fifty-five at the time too. *A stroke at fifty-five...*

The doctors said he'd had the condition building up for years, but I believed it was the stress. It had to be.

He'd be so happy if I were to get him the house of his dreams. Maybe somewhere on the coast. He'd always loved the beach. He loved fishing, so I could get him a little boat too.

"Dad would be really proud of me," I mused.

"Honey, he's already proud of you. This isn't about that. He'd just be able to get better in a happy place, without the stress of worrying so much. I know he also feels bad that you had to give up your career for him, so… your being able to set up your business properly would be amazing."

I smiled wider at that. It really would be amazing. "I'm scared to dream, Lana. Every time I get to this point where I think this could be it for me and I could really do this, something happens."

"Not this time. I feel like this is the moment for you. You could even start looking for places for your new business."

I hadn't told her that I'd found the perfect place. "Look at this."

I pulled out my phone and found the listing on the commercial real estate website.

There it was. Situated in the middle of Santa

Monica Blvd. was my place. My dream place for my business.

Number One to Four Santa Monica Blvd. Right now, it was empty. It had been a recruitment consultancy firm, so the place was set up in exactly the way I wanted it.

Marble floors, shelve spaces, and office spaces. Cream and beige colors adorned the walls with gold trimmings. Classy and sexy. It was me.

"My gosh, girl, yassss! Georgie, this is you. This really is you for damn sure. You could buy it straight up with that money." She nodded her approval.

"I could." The place was selling for four hundred and fifty thousand.

I thought maybe I'd see how much Dad's place would cost first, then I'd probably make an appointment to view it. There were some refurbishments being done on the back roof before sale, and it was listed as being available for viewings in four weeks.

The other day when I'd looked at it, my heart melted. I fell in love with the place and wanted it. Now, it kind of felt like it could happen.

"You know, I think this is all amazing for you. Nothing else matters, Georgie. You deserve this." Lana rubbed her hands together. "Also, I think this could be fun. It's actually *going* to be fun. Screw the rest of the concerns you have. You should be the you, you were back in New York."

Now there was a thought. I was so glamourous back in New York.

Facials every week. Hair and nails done like I was going to a party every day. The clothes I had too were all so elaborate, so much so that when I moved here, I was able to auction some of my designer stuff and get an easy fifteen thousand just for my clothes.

New York was an exciting city to live in. L.A. always was too, more than New York, so to think I digressed was weird.

It was the case of having to roll with the situation.

I hadn't known that Dad was back here with no money. He'd kept it all from me, that he'd given all of it to Angelica. Apparently, she'd been in another life-or-death situation where she needed to be bailed out. A hundred grand that time. Or else, her head would have been delivered to him in a jiffy bag.

That was the sort of things that had happened over the years. That last time though was the worst because Dad wasn't able to bounce back. He'd lowered his insurance plans, and then *boom* he had that stroke, and that was it. It took him down, and me too.

"Me in New York. Pat didn't know that side of me." I smiled.

"You should introduce him to that, Georgie. I saw a

little bit of you the other day when you went to meet Marsha. Honey, those heels aren't for business meetings." She chuckled. "They're for seriously hot men."

"He'll see a little bit of me. I agreed to twelve percent of that version of me."

She gave me a curious stare. "What do you mean, you agreed? And twelve percent?"

"I was just being silly with him. Trying to loosen up because he was being difficult about taking me to The Globe for 1940s Night."

"And the conversation was?" She flicked her wrists over and looked at me with expectancy, waiting for me to elaborate.

"It was just that. I was basically telling him how lucky he was, and my actual husband would be getting ninety percent of me. Damn sexy me, and we wouldn't leave the bedroom."

She burst out laughing. "Oh my gosh, you said that to him?"

"Yes."

"What did he say?"

I laughed because that had been such a ridiculous conversation. "He asked for twelve percent. I told him he'd get five, but he insisted on twelve percent."

Her glossy pink lips parted, and surprise suffused her pretty face. "Oh my God, he said that."

"Yes, but that was such a Pat thing to say."

"No, it was not. Girl, you put that bedroom image of you in the man's mind, and he asked for twelve percent. Watch him get fifty, then *seventy-five*." She widened her eyes.

"Lana, please, we were just messing around."

She cleared her throat. "Sweetie, you know in this plan of yours, you have to kiss him, right?"

I held her gaze and bit the inside of my lip as I nodded slowly. I knew that part.

The kiss. It had been on my mind all night as we planned and after I left his place to go to mine. It was thinking of the kiss that sent me home because last night was the kind of night when I usually would have stayed at his.

"I was doing a prospective plan for all of this and thinking of all the things we could do. I got stuck with the kiss." I brought my knees up and hugged them to my chest.

"How do you even plan a kiss?" She smirked.

"I don't think you can, but I have to. Like everything I do, I'm going to make sure this works. I'm not passing on a big dream of mine only to fail. So, I want us to look like we had a gradual but fast progression to that moment when he proposes to me."

"I hear ya, and that sounds good. You know what though?" She tilted her head to the side. "This is all so good because people would definitely believe that you two would fall for each other. So, that being said, why don't you plan all the stuff like your little events and public appearances, then… you could let the other stuff, like kissing, come naturally."

I continued to stare at her, wondering if she was being serious. "Naturally? You think Pat and I will kiss naturally?"

"Yes, I happen to think that. Of course, I do. Have I ever been wrong?"

I took a moment to think. She actually hadn't ever been wrong. "No, but it doesn't mean you'll be right about this."

"I think you're finding it hard to kiss him because when you fantasize about kissing him, it's wild and passionate and it's the kind you don't want people to see. Yassss, hunni," she teased, giving me an accusatory stare.

"That is so not true."

"Oh, stop with the prudishness. Georgie, life has thrown you crap for a long time. Have fun with this. It's almost like a no-strings-attached relationship. You could do whatever you want for the benefit of making this fake engagement look believable. It just depends on what you want to do."

"Lana, what are you telling me to do?" I shook my head at her.

"Milk it and have fun. Fun in whatever sense that means. Basically, do everything I would do."

We both started laughing at that.

Everything she would do would be *everything*. This girl would hop right into bed with Pat and devour the man before he could take his next breath.

It was just the joke of the universe that it was me and not her who got this gig.

I couldn't help but wonder though…

If I could really be like that.

God, what the hell was I going to have to do in public?

CHAPTER 10

Patterson

DAY ONE OF THE PLAN...
I didn't know what Georgie had up her sleeve today, but it was day one. We'd start with today and work or way across to next Friday.

I sat opposite Dad in the staff restaurant.

He wanted a quick breakfast meeting because something came up with one of the projects we were working on.

We were known for the bizarre, but yesterday, one of the construction workers came across a mummified corpse while they were knocking down one of the old buildings on the East Coast.

Of course, that meant work on the project had to stop immediately and the police and forensics team got involved. It was on the news too.

Dad wanted to brainstorm ideas on what we could do with the clients who'd purchased the property.

"They're gonna lose thousands. *We're* gonna lose thousands because work has to stop until the police finish doing what they need to. I wondered if it would look good on our part if we offer some form of discount during this time." His salt and pepper brows arched, and he looked concerned.

That was his problem. He might have taken this company to a place no one could have imagined, creating jobs for the whole family, but his decisions sometimes threw me.

"Dad, it's force majeure, act of nature, act of the unpredictable. Basically, not our fault so we shouldn't act like it is. Bryce Hammelson isn't exactly broke." Bryce had been a long-term client of ours, and he was of the same caliber as us in the finance department. The man was filthy rich with the kind of old money we actually didn't have. He didn't need the type of compassion Dad wanted to offer. "Also, the place should have been surveyed properly."

My understanding was that they hadn't used our

surveyors. They used a different company. Chances were, we might not have found anything to lead us to the body, but there was a chance we could have found it.

I heard it was one of the foremen who'd spotted a hole in the ground. Digging through led them there. We would have spotted that.

"You don't think it's a good idea to do something?"

"Dad, you don't want to know what I think." At least we were talking business and not about my problem. That was okay by me.

"Actually, I do. That's the reason for this meeting."

"Okay, well, here's what I think. We don't need to lose money with them by waiting for the police work to be done. I would reschedule. I get that we've known Bryce forever, but business is business. We have clients on a waiting list. We can divert our contractors to a smaller project and resume work with him when all is said and done."

Dad looked at me. "Boy, you seem to be getting better and better than me at this every day."

"Am I now?" I couldn't hide the sarcasm in my voice.

He chuckled. "Still upset with me?"

"Really, Dad?"

"Patterson Flynn, don't be mad at your old man for wanting to see his kid married and settled down. I'm more than ready to be a grandfather now. I'm not getting any younger. I'm seventy years old, son. Humor me."

I rolled my eyes at him. Great, now we were talking about kids. I'd better be careful. He could add in a baby too. "You have nieces and nephews and great nieces and nephews. You can have all the fun in the world with them."

"It's not the same. I want to be called grandfather. The same as my father was. Or grandpa. I want to wear a stupid jumper at Christmas with the words printed on it. Heck, I even want a Christmas card and birthday cards. *To Grandpa, love from, the babies*." He chuckled.

I sighed and was ready to tell him to adopt and give himself the title, but the sight of Georgie coming through the door caught my attention.

And it wasn't because I was glad to be saved by her presence.

It was what she wore.

A black business dress with lacey sleeves showed off curves I didn't even know the woman had. She always looked good on a workday, but she mostly wore shirts and pant suits. She also mostly had her hair tied back, and if it was down, it was that just-washed look that carried a wave or two.

The woman who walked toward me had had her hair styled into long, graceful waves that shined and sparkled as she got closer.

She wore hot pink lipstick and large diamond studs in her ear.

This was definitely the best I'd ever seen her look.

Dad glanced over his shoulder and saw her, and saw me watching her.

He gave me a curious look but diverted his attention to her when she skipped up to us.

"Morning I'm so sorry to disturb your meeting. I just had to talk to my amazing boss about something really important." She beamed, returning Dad's smile.

"Pet, you never have to apologize," Dad replied.

Plan in motion. There wasn't a bad thing Georgie could ever do, and both my parents addressed her just like that when they spoke to her.

Pet, dear, love… Those were some of the names they gave her.

I definitely had this in the bag.

"Thank you so much," she cooed in that oh so gracious voice that would melt anyone like hot butter over freshly made cornbread.

I stood up and moved with her over to the booths. I noticed she stopped just in Dad's line of sight too.

"You look really good," I complimented.

"I had to dig deep to find this dress and pray it still fit me. You should be grateful." She instantly swapped to the Georgie I was used to.

"I like this." I reached out and touched her hair. It was so soft I could have continued to stroke it.

She leaned in closer, and I suddenly became aware of the closeness. And that perfume.

"Damn... you smell good," I mused, leaning in closer to smell her better.

"Stay there. Your Dad is watching us," she whispered. Then she started laughing at something but I didn't know what.

"What? What are we laughing at?"

"Just think of something funny and laugh with me." She giggled.

This was hard to do on the spot. What the hell was I supposed to think of? I laughed, and it sounded fake.

"You sound terrible." She frowned while she continued to laugh. "Think of something funny. Like when you fell off the boat because you were too drunk. Or like when you slipped on that chicken bone and fell over." She was actually laughing for real now, and I started laughing too because I remembered that while I was embarrassed to no end on both those occasions, I'd laughed because she was hilarious to watch when she was laughing at me instead of helping me.

"You're the terrible one."

She pressed her hand to my chest and lingered there. "Touch my face and pretend you think my skin is soft."

I did, and I didn't have to pretend because her skin *was* soft. "Wow."

"Good, enough. Now you have permission to stare at my ass as I walk away. Meet me for lunch later at Starbucks." She gave me a deliciously devilish smile.

I was stuck on the word 'ass' and looked indeed as she sauntered away.

I knew there was supposed to be a point when I should have stopped looking, but I couldn't tear my eyes away from the perfect view of her ass leaving me.

It made my damn cock stir in my pants.

I watched her until she got to the door and glanced over her shoulder with a quick smile. I had to wonder why it was no one had pointed out that my little PA had the most perfect ass I'd ever seen.

When I turned back to Dad, I saw that he'd watched that whole thing, including me staring at Georgie's ass. I would have felt some ounce of triumph if I'd been able to steady my arousal.

I went back to him and sat down.

"Everything okay?" he asked. I could hear the curiosity in his tone.

"Yes, sure. Of course."

"Oh good. Always nice to see her. She's a great girl." Dad nodded like he was trying to tell me something.

"I know." I more than knew that.

No one had to tell me that part.

What I also knew was this: the seeds were sown.

The days that followed were just like that.

Either Georgie or I would do something to draw attention to ourselves. Always the right attention.

By the following Friday, we had Dad definitely suspicious of our behavior, the office gossip swearing we were dating and having some secret affair, and people making various bets.

What was good though was we'd done it in ways that looked subtle and tactful. It looked like something was happening, but people couldn't be certain.

To Dad, it looked like something was definitely in the works, but not some sort of scam. Which, essentially, it was.

Friday, however, came.

The big day. The big day for more than one reason.

Big date tonight, but a big meeting too with Dad and Hudson, who'd arrived this morning.

As far as I knew, Dad had a meeting with him earlier when he'd arrived.

Georgie told me she saw them together, and when she checked Dad's schedule, there was a big old meeting booked out in there for an hour and a half.

As a company, we all got together a few times a year

to discuss certain things, but this was outside that. So, I was willing to bet the cat was out of the bag that I wasn't just going to be handed the company.

Fuck. Hudson was such an asshole.

He really was. The part that made him so bad was, he was a prick.

He treated his staff like shit, and he treated family like shit too.

Dad might be worshiping him and singing his praises because Hudson was a family man, but I wished he would ask him where he spent the night Christmas Eve, when he called in to say he was snowed in in Colorado. Or who that woman was nibbling on his neck when we went to Vegas for Donny's thirtieth birthday.

From where I'd stood, it definitely was not Melanie, his wife of ten years.

One thing I was not was a cheater. No. Not me.

It wasn't my style, and I wouldn't entertain the thought. Not even with this fake marriage in the stars for me. The way Georgie and I would get divorced was this...

Irreconcilable differences.

Simple as that.

The door opened, and she walked in with a bright smile on her face.

This was how I liked her.

She waltzed up to where I sat behind my desk, ponytail bouncing, adjusting her bag on her shoulder. Today, she wore a navy-blue camisole top and a pencil skirt that showed off her golden legs.

She looked really, really good.

"Get up. I need your computer." She demanded waving her hand over me.

"What?" She looked like she was off somewhere, and I was hoping she'd come to the meeting with me. "Where are you going, baby?"

"I'm leaving for the day. I have to get ready for tonight," she bubbled.

"We're meeting at eight. It's not even two yet."

She looked me up and down and smirked. "I'm leaving for the day. I have things to do."

"Georgie, I wanted you to come to the meeting with me." I really didn't want to sound as desperate as that sounded.

"So your creepy cousin can stare at my tits and try to proposition me like he always does? Hell no. You're my pre-boyfriend now, and I'm putting my foot down."

I held up my hand to stop her from ranting. What was she saying to me about Hudson?

My blood started to simmer. "Say that again, slowly this time, so I can really hear you."

"Pat, you heard me. I think I have grounds to refuse

to attend any meeting now that we're dating." She folded her arms and nodded.

"Georgie, you had grounds before we were dating. Why didn't you say something?" I would have kicked his ass if she had. In fact, I was going to ask him about it today when I saw him.

"I thought you knew. Last time he was here, he looked at me from across the meeting room, then looked at my breasts and licked his lips."

I balled my fists and punched the table. It hurt my knuckles, but not enough to affect me.

"Fucking bastard. Georgie, you should have said something."

"Well, now you know. I soldiered through out of respect for you, but it's time to change things up. I will not be attending any meetings I don't need to with that man. Full stop."

I was sitting on, ready to hit someone, but I had to admit her quirky, fiery ways cooled me off. Just a little though. I was still going to ask Hudson what he thought he was playing at when I saw him.

"You don't have to. Where are you going though? And why's it going to take that many hours for you to get ready? We're just going to a jazz club."

"Never mind that. I want to look like a million dollars. Now, get up. Clock's ticking, and mama need some tit tape."

Tit tape?

I narrowed my eyes at her. "What did you just say?"

"Pat, get up. My computer crashed, so I couldn't get my discount code."

I got up and humored her just to see what she was up to.

She sat down in my chair and started tapping away at my keyboard.

I furrowed my brows when she brought up my emails, and I saw that not only had she'd signed me up to get ten percent off my first order at Perky Tits, but she'd entered me in for a giveaway where the grand prize was a lifetime supply of Perky Tit tape.

"Baby, what the hell is this?"

She cut me a glance. "Tit tape, Pat."

"And the reason you signed me up for tit tape is?"

"So we could both get a discount for me to use and double my chances of winning a lifetime supply."

I looked at her, and she bit the inside of her lip trying not to laugh. She looked away and wrote down the discount code to use in the store. When she looked back to me, she still had that coy, mischievous expression on her face.

"What kind of dress are you wearing later?"

"A nice one."

"What kind of dress requires all this?"

"The kind you don't wear a bra with." She pouted.

I don't know who told me to look down at her breasts, but I made the mistake of doing so, to my misfortune.

My gaze landed on her fully rounded breasts that were enunciated in that top of hers that showed off just the right amount of cleavage.

How in the hell had I not seen those before? Considering I was a breast man, I didn't know how those escaped me.

She snapped her fingers in front of my face and smiled the way a temptress would.

"Eyes up. Those aren't for you," she cooed with a sexy giggle. She stepped closer, and the sun shimmered off her warm brown skin. Whatever she had on it today made her sparkle.

She pressed her finger to my chest, and her smile widened.

"Is there anything that's going to be for me?" That was something I would have never asked her.

She shook her head and ran that finger over my chest. "No."

"So, what do I get for twelve percent? You haven't said."

She must have got me hooked on some spell because she suddenly waved my card wallet in front of my face. My car wallet that had been in my jacket pocket.

I didn't even know or see when she got it.

BELLA FONTAINE & KHARDINE GRAY

She smiled at her trickery and my further misfortune.

"You'll see. I'll try not to spend too much."

"Hey." I tried to take the wallet back, but she moved away.

"Hey yourself. I'm enjoying the perks while I can. I also don't see why I have to pay for anything else as long as I live."

I laughed. I had to. "Fine, go knock yourself out." I wanted something though. "You remember how you slapped me last week?"

"Yes."

"The sting is still there. I need you to kiss it better." I tapped my cheek and bent down. "Come on now, baby. Don't keep me waiting."

A playful smile lifted the corners of her lips, and she leaned in to plant a kiss on my cheek.

When her soft, soft lips brushed over my skin first then stayed there, it did something to me. It made my skin tingle and warmth rush over my cheeks.

Damn... if her kissing me on my cheek felt like that, then what would her lips feel like?

She reached for my jaw, and I almost thought she was going to answer that question, but she didn't. She stared at me long and hard.

"Don't be late later, Pat."

With that one-shoulder sassy shrug, she sauntered

away, wiggling her hips in that short pencil skirt that drew my attention straight to her perfect ass.

Perfect ass, fully rounded breasts that made me not want to look away.

What the hell was wrong with me?

This was my Georgie?

My Georgie, who just happened to be a woman. It was as if someone had wiped smoke from my eyes and I'd just realized that.

CHAPTER 11

Patterson

"It's always great to meet like this as family." Dad smiled, looking from Hudson to me.

Hudson gave me a long, hard stare. The asshole, he couldn't even pretend he liked me. Then there was Dad sitting in front of us, at the head of the table, completely clueless. It was like someone had covered his eyes with a blindfold and he couldn't see shit.

I looked at Hudson and had to seriously contemplate this scenario.

This was the guy Dad thought was a better fit than me to take over the whole empire.

"Could we get to the point of this meeting, please," I cut in. "I have things to do." I hoped that sounded as rude as I intended.

Hudson smiled while Dad looked embarrassed.

"Patterson, please," Dad fumed. "Don't be so stand-offish. Hudson has joined us today. I have told him the situation at hand, and I think it's important that we meet and talk since you'll be working together one way or the other."

"I have no problem with talking," Hudson stated, then looked about the room. "Thought your little PA would be here to take minutes."

I crackled my knuckles and stared him down.

I'd do it...

Hit him. Hit him right here, no matter who was watching and no matter what it looked like.

"You won't be seeing her today," I answered.

"What a shame."

"Indeed."

"Anyway," Dad cut in. "Patterson, Hudson, I have opened the floor to the both of you. Patterson, you are my son and obviously get first pick of the empire if you fulfill the demands I gave you personally. Hudson, as my brother's oldest son, I felt it right to offer you the chance too because of the wonderful work you've been doing in New York and Chicago. You will both know my decision by the evening of the fundraiser. Do you have any questions?"

I simply looked at Dad. The only thing this was to me was an embarrassment. It seemed like he hadn't given Hudson specifics, but I was still very embarrassed by this.

He could have at least given me a chance first to fail, to essentially fail, before showing me up like this.

This might all look kosher to him and like a great idea, but really, it wasn't.

I'd be damned if I had a son and could do this to him. No matter my reasons. This was complete shit.

"I have none." I shook my head.

"No questions for me. I do have some news though, on a potential investment in The Dominican Republic," Hudson announced then with his bright self-satisfied look directed my way and gave me a smile. "I'm thinking of buying a chain of hotels that are up for sale. They need doing up, but we could make a pretty penny from the acquisition if we take it."

Dad looked so proud and pleased. "I like that."

"Well, you know me. Always on the lookout for new business ideas to expand the company and stay strong. I figured we start there and take on the entire Caribbean. We could rival Sandals."

He definitely talked big. The thing was, it wasn't a bad idea.

"Let's make an appointment to talk about that. I like that idea," Dad said, nodding, then looked to me.

I didn't need to enter this pissing contest, but I wasn't going to allow this prick to have one over on me. He thought he was hot shit talking like that with his ideas.

I was about to serve him his sauce.

"Wonderful idea, Hudson, sure. I'm guessing you want me to acknowledge that, and Dad, I think it's great you want to discuss things further. I think you definitely should. It's absolutely something to be looked into with the opportunity to buy the hotel chain. May I suggest, however, that you don't approach this with the mindset of rivalling Sandals. Sandals is considered the jewel of the Caribbean. When you piss on other people's territory, it's not always good. Especially when there's nothing wrong with what they're doing. Harmony works better in situations like that. McDonalds, KFC, and Burger King all sell food. They don't rival each other or try to compete. In fact, they can even be on the same street or in the same food complex and still do well. How they work is this: they allow the people to decide what they want. Each has a uniqueness about them that allows them to coexist together and still make a fuck-load of money. Taste and options. The question you ask yourself should be, what can we bring to the table that will help us flourish in a market that already exists and people love?"

Even I knew that sounded fucking amazing.

The look on Hudson's face was classic, and Dad looked utterly impressed and surprised. I didn't know why he'd need to be surprised. I was his son and took after him in brains and brawn. That was the kind of thing he would say. I'd just proved I'd been listening over the long, long years I'd worked for him.

He nodded and looked at me with pride.

"This..." He held up his finger and continued to stare. "That is everything."

"Thank you, Dad."

"I'd love for you two to spend the next half an hour together, just you two, to talk," Dad suggested. "It's important to me that you two talk and get along. There are so many solid ideas and talent in this family, and I love that you two are born leaders. It really works well. That was how my brothers and I were. You guys are cousins."

Dad stood. I really wished he wouldn't leave us. All he said sounded like a good idea and would work on normal cousins who could indeed get a long or at least be cordial with one another, but we'd never been like that.

But... yes, let's talk. I knew I had shit to discuss with him about Georgie. As for anything else, I wasn't interested in hearing any more of his ideas, and I didn't want to know what he thought about anything. He could think that it would be a good idea to purchase the fucking sun, for all I cared.

Dad gave us one last look before leaving.

I kept my gaze trained on Hudson, however. When the door closed, his face changed into the devil he was. I had to give him credit for keeping up appearances while Dad was around. This was what used to happen when we were kids. I was two years younger than him, and back then, I was scrawny until I hit fourteen.

I was like a rake with long legs. Then I suddenly bulked out. Prior to that, he used to beat me up every chance he got. That was just for existing.

Then I grew a pair, and the muscles came with it. That year, just before my fifteenth birthday, I broke his nose and his arm when he came for me.

"You think you're hot shit just because you're his son, don't you?" he asked.

"No, I'm hot shit because I'm fabulous." I didn't mind sounding like a self-centered bastard when it came to him. "You know what I said made better sense than what you said. Accept it and deal, prick."

"If you were that fabulous, I wouldn't be here. I'm guessing Uncle Richard saw sense and realized the worthless asshole his son was. It's been way overdue."

"Don't you worry about that, or me."

"You're gone the minute he hands the company over to me, Patterson." He nodded. I'd guessed that was going to happen the minute Dad told me he was a candidate. I didn't plan to work here anymore if that happened. "I don't care that this is a family business. I won't work with you in any capacity. I will take that little pretty little PA of yours though. I'd bet her pussy tastes as sweet as she looks and that mouth of hers will look good on my cock. I—"

Oh no, no, no.

That was quite enough. I'd only allowed him to say as much as he had because I wanted to hear him speak his mind, so I'd be justified in what I was about to do.

I practically stepped over the desk and grabbed him around his neck before he knew what was happening. He tried to punch me, but I landed a fist smack in his face, stunning him. I moved with him right over to the wall where I shoved him against it.

We were practically the same height. I was an inch taller, that was all. So, he could have tried to take me. If only he had an equal amount or more muscle than me.

"You fucking dog. You absolute fucking dog." I had to bridle my anger because I had a good mind to punch him again. "You have a wife and three kids. Babies. You have no respect for any of them. Don't you dare talk about my girl that way ever. Don't even look at her."

Despite the odds definitely not in his favor, he started laughing. "So, you really are sleeping with her?"

I fisted him in his stomach, and he doubled over. "That is not your concern."

I would have cleared that up, but I didn't.

Let him believe that. Georgie might have come up with all these ideas to create a buzz. Well, I think this would get the buzz going real good. It would stir the pot.

Not that I defended my girl's honor because of this crazy engagement. I would have done it with or without it.

In fact, I would have probably messed him up a little more just for that last comment.

"We're done here. Discussion over. Nice talking to you, as always," I sneered and walked away, leaving him to unwind himself.

I decided to go straight home. I didn't have any meetings left for the day. It was all contracts I needed to sign off on some of my new and existing clients, but that could wait until Monday.

I was too pissed to calm myself down for that type of mundane work. I hated admin anyway, and that part had to be done by me.

I went home, worked out for an hour to burn off some stress, and then I detoxed my mind of Hudson and Dad. Tonight would have probably seen me hooking up with Phoebe again, but she was a woman of the past.

It was funny I'd actually cleansed my mind of all the hosts of women I knew the second Georgie said to me *If you're with me, you're with me.*

I wouldn't forget that. Of all the things she could have asked me for, she said no whores and no bed friends, and I got it. I understood. It was out of respect to consider the person you were with. I could never disappoint her in that way.

I didn't know how Hudson did it so effortlessly.

That damn Hudson, and it wasn't just him either. Most of my cousins were like that. They cheated on their wives.

Why? Because my uncles were like that too. Or had been.

Dad was the only one of the four brothers who'd run this company who'd been loyal to his wife and set the example, which no one else followed. Craig, Dad's older brother, was Hudson's father, and he was notorious for cheating.

No one spoke about it though, and the wives all stayed, all of them putting up with the shit.

It made me sick and enraged me when they started talking about me. Like I was the bad seed. I was the bad seed because I was reckless and wild and couldn't be tamed. Better to be that than a cheater.

Anyhow, it was time to switch focus.

I got dressed in a white button-down shirt and a black Boss suit. I thought I'd go with something I knew since I was going to be out of my element at The Globe. And 40s night?

God, I didn't know how I'd ended up agreeing, but it was Georgie. She would get me to do anything, it seemed.

The minute I stepped inside the club, I was enveloped by the smooth music that took me right back to my days spent with my grandparents.

They used to dance together, every day, all day if allowed, to that smooth music that seemed to speak to the soul. It wasn't never that I didn't like it. I just didn't take to it, I guess. It didn't help that Grandfather always insisted on teaching me how to dance.

He always said you had to know how to do it and save your best moves for the woman who'll appreciate it. He'd been so different before Grandma died. More sentimental, more appreciative of life.

After her death, he was just a different version of Hugh Hefner.

The place was packed with the type of crowd I'd expected. Young and old. People from the forties, children of the forties, and fans of the forties. And bingo, I spotted a few people in the mix who knew me and knew my family. Dad's friends from the country club. A few of their sons and their wives and girlfriends dotted here and there.

Most of them looked surprised to see me here, but I tipped my head for curt nods of hello as I made my way through the dancing crowd.

Everyone had made an effort to dress up in period wear, and it really looked like we could have been in a scene from 1945. Especially with some of the men wearing old military uniforms from the war. The women looked their parts in glamorous gowns, hair and makeup styled just like then too.

I felt like I'd just walked onto the set of one of the films my grandparents used to watch. I definitely had to give them all credit for the effort.

I might have been out of my element in the sense that this wasn't my usual thing, but I liked it for the sentiment it carried for me.

I went to the bar and stood by it. This was where I was supposed to meet Georgie.

I'd wanted to pick her up, but she insisted on meeting me here.

And she was late.

Miss 'Don't be late later' was late herself.

It was eight fifteen, and she was supposed to be here at eight.

I shook my head and was about to order a drink

when my eyes landed on a very, very beautiful woman coming down the stairs from the main entrance.

Her beauty was such that it drew eyes to her.

The elegant white gown that caressed her body looked stark against her honey-colored skin. It dipped low in the front and scooped across her perfect cleavage.

With her hair rolled up in a classic forties style, it showed off the elegance of her neck, sleek and long, perfect for kissing.

Smoky eyes framed with thick dark lashes stood out along with blood red lips.

I must have been looking for too long because she smiled at me and started heading in my direction.

Remembering my vivid promise to Georgie, I looked away and focused my attention on the bottle of gin on the counter behind the bar.

It was just the one woman, and all I did was look. I'd tamed myself before I thought anything else, and to be fair, everyone else was looking at her too.

I told myself the same thing when she came up to me and rested her dainty hand on my arm.

I looked at her, about to tell her that I was waiting for someone, but I froze when I realized she was my Georgie.

"Pat," she spoke.

I heard her, but I didn't hear her, and it wasn't because the music was too loud.

It was a mellow beat that allowed us to carry a conversation. Besides, over by the bar, the volume was turned to low so people could place their orders and still talk to each other.

"Georgie..." I had to narrow my eyes, and then I realized I was staring and it was weird.

"I'm sorry I'm late. The taxi driver was weird, kept asking for my number." She giggled.

"Please tell me that doesn't surprise you. Look at you."

Her smile widened. "You like?"

She twirled around. I wished she didn't because the back of the dress scooped low too so that it took the curve of her body and sat low, just below the small of her back, flowing down her gorgeous ass and down her legs.

Then, God help me, there was a slit on each side.

It was the sort of dress to torture a man who wasn't supposed to be having seriously wild sexual thoughts about his best friend.

She flashed me a dazzling smile when she saw my face.

"You look beautiful," I told her.

"This was how I used to dress back in New York," she mused with an air of reminisce in her voice.

"Well, hello, New York Georgia, I hope you stay in L.A." I said that showing far too much emotion as I held her gaze. Emotion that included guilt too.

"I think I missed her, so she may stay."

I thought she was beautiful no matter what she did, but her tonight was obviously the real her. I was largely to blame for her change in image. She was always doing stuff for me. All around the clock. What time did she have for herself, and her father?

One more thing to add to my list of things I had to make up to her.

"So, this is twelve percent?"

She chuckled. "Thirty."

"Thirty percent for me?"

"Thirty percent for you." She nodded.

A song I recognized started playing. My grandparents always used to play this one. It was their wedding song. They got married at the end of the war.

It was called *It's Been a Long, Long Time.*

Another sentiment. As I looked at Georgie, something warmed my heart. It was like learning or knowing something suddenly.

The dancing, the song. This was the only woman I knew who'd appreciate me dancing with her.

"Dance with me," I said, holding that gaze of her beautiful brown eyes that looked shocked to hear the words coming out of my mouth.

"*Dance?* You dance? To this music?"

I took her hand, her small hand, into mine and brought it up to my lips to kiss.

"I dance. There's a lot about me you don't know," I stated with a wink.

"It looks that way."

CHAPTER 12

Georgie

HOW COULD we have been dancing for hours?

I couldn't believe we were even dancing.

Me and Pat...

Pat and I...

Dancing amongst the sea of people, then practically by ourselves as the people started leaving.

Dancing close now with both of his arms around me as I rested my head on his chest and my hands on his wide shoulders.

The music seemed to take us to a place we'd never

gone before, and all I could think about was this moment we were spending together.

I loved anything from the forties but never had anyone to share it with. This was an event I would have wished I could go to and dance at exactly like this, but it would have been a thing I hoped for and passed on because I never had anyone to go with.

Not till tonight, and boy, was I ever glad I'd suggested this.

I thought I'd have a night of him griping about how this wasn't his type of place and how he would have preferred to go to one of the trendier clubs. Then talking about how it was more for people of his grandparents' age.

This man had, however, shocked me to death.

He shocked me in the hours we spent dancing, to one song after the other. Rhythm poured through his body, flowing into mine, and all I was aware of was the music and the steady rhythm of his heart.

The lights blinked above us, and the music faded to a soft beat.

It was only then that I looked up and around and noticed that it really was just us.

Pat did too, then looked down at me with a smile.

A guy dressed in a suit and bow tie went up on the stage, where they normally had live bands playing, and smiled at us.

"Thank you all for coming," he said into the microphone. "My couple on the floor, I wish now we had a competition for the life of the party and the last ones standing. Thank you for the beauty in your dancing." He clapped, and the remaining people around us clapped too.

It suddenly dawned on me that I'd actually forgotten the purpose of tonight.

We were here to create this buzz to start our fake relationship.

Something tugged on my heart at the thought.

Sadness. But I shouldn't feel sad. There were so many reasons why I shouldn't.

"Thank you," we both said to the man, who bowed before exiting the stage.

The music stopped completely. I returned my focus to Pat, who was still holding me.

"I don't know what time it is." He grinned.

"Me neither."

"You must be tired."

I shook my head. "I think I should be, but I'm not."

"Let's go back to mine for drinks."

"I have that wine from Paris you got me for my birthday," I suddenly remembered.

He widened his eyes when I said that. "Woman, how the hell do you still have that? We're going to yours."

He took my hand and led me away.

We got to my place at nearly one a.m.

"I'll go change and sort out the drinks," I said, slipping out of my heels.

He caught my arm before I could go into my room and pulled me back. "No, the dress stays. You stay like this. I'll allow you to take off the killer heels on account of us dancing for over four hours, but the dress stays."

I laughed. "You'll allow me?"

"Yes, baby, I'm calling dibs on still being the boss of you. So, you stay like this, and I soak up the last thirty percent of you. When that sun comes up, you can do whatever you want with the dress. Within reason."

I laughed again. "Does this mean I get more me time in the week so I can look good for you?"

I giggled as he took my hand and pulled me out to the terrace.

He picked me up and set me on top of the table while he made a show of bowing to me and planting kisses on top of my feet.

"You are so crazy, Pat."

His hair fell forward over his eye, and he shrugged out of his jacket.

"You get whatever time you want for you." He placed one last kiss on my right foot.

"Pat, you do realize there's no one around to see us. No one will see you kissing my feet."

"I want you to see it. Besides, there's nobody seeing anything up here. I love you, but I hate your apartment, baby."

He was always saying that to me.

"It works for what I need it for."

"Either you come live with me, or I'll buy you a new place." He slid into the wicker chair and sat forward.

He'd given me that offer many times, but I refused every single time.

"No, this place works for me."

"Georgie, you're at my place more than you are here. Imagine the fun." In the soft glow of the overhead lights his eyes lit up and sparkled.

"Pat, that is completely one sided. Imagine it, if I lived with you, aside from the fact that people would swear blindly that we're sleeping together, I'd be cooking and cleaning. Chasing after you and your craziness all the time. Then there are the bed friends and bed groupies I'd have to deal with."

The spark in his eyes dimmed the minute I said that. "No. There are no bed friends and bed groupies. Remember, I promised. So, maybe you could... you could pretend that never happened. Like you never saw me like that."

This was a different side too. A side I'd never seen to him before.

"Pretend?"

"Yeah, just pretend. I hate that you think badly of me."

I laughed. "Pat, when I was cleaning up and covering your back, making sure you didn't get your dates or women mixed up, didn't it cross your mind that I'd think badly of you then?"

He opened his mouth to say something but stopped and sighed. "Can we just, maybe… probably put all that in the past and start fresh? Learn more about each other. Like New York. You never talk about that."

I smiled. "That's true, and I guess we can. I would like to hear more about this dancing. I didn't know you could dance." I tucked a stray strand of hair behind my ear. "It was nice. It made tonight more than I thought it would be. I'm sorry. I know it was supposed to be more of a show, and I should have done more to show off or something to create that buzz. I just got lost in the music. And us dancing."

He smiled at that. "Is that a plus in your book, something good to hold on to about me? Something good you can remember me for?"

I chuckled. "Absolutely. Where'd you learn to dance like that?"

"My grandfather. He and my grandmother used to dance like that all the time."

That was sweet, hearing him say that. Normally when he spoke of his grandfather, it was mostly all the bad, unsavory stuff.

"I could have danced all night."

"You tired?"

"I should be, but I'm not." I smiled.

He pulled out his phone, tapped on the screen to bring up his playlists, and to my surprise found the song we'd first danced to tonight. It was my favorite.

"How about a few more songs, we drink that whole bottle of wine, then call it a night?"

My God, this was beyond weird, but I couldn't resist the bubble of excitement that filtered through me at the thought of dancing with him again.

"I'd love that."

He took my hand, and I slid off the table right into his arms.

Just the way we'd been on the dance floor when there were so many eyes on us.

Now, it was just us.

CHAPTER 13

Georgie

HE WAS GONE when I woke up later in the day, but there was a message on my phone inviting me to lunch at the docks.

I thought I'd check in on Dad first before heading there.

Dad seemed a little better than he'd looked last week. Dr. Thompson had scheduled me in to meet with him and Dad on Monday to go over the plans for everything. All day yesterday, I tried to not worry because I knew I was taking steps to fix the situation.

What I hated was that time waited for no one. At

least I knew I could pay for his surgery. It was probably the sort of thing I could pay for in installments with my current salary and savings, as they were, if it happened in the next two weeks. But I prayed that it was the sort of thing that could wait—Lord willing—until a little after the end of the month. I didn't know how things would work out, but I wasn't exactly going to be checking off the dates until I got my million.

Thinking about it now didn't feel right.

Dad was sitting on the sofa watching a re-run of a basketball game.

As always, he looked happy to see me. Always greeting me with that smile that brightened his face.

I missed living with him sometimes. I loved the comfort he gave me and that warm presence. We both knew, however, that I needed my space. He did too. Especially in our tiny apartments that didn't exactly make one good one.

"Hey, baby girl. You look happy today," he noted when I gave him a kiss on his cheek.

"I am," I replied. I guess I felt happier than I had been in a very long time.

Last week, I came right round to this whole idea of being Pat's fake wife, fake fiancé first.

I guess fake girlfriend. It still felt weird, and I was having the same trouble with it sinking in, but it really was something I could make myself move past.

Two million dollars to pretend.

It was just that last night had been no pretense.

Not from me anyway, and Pat dancing with me at my place out on the balcony for hours later was no pretense either.

At least I didn't think it was. It hadn't felt like it.

"What's happening with you? There's a glow about you that I'm liking. We haven't spoken about anything that wasn't problems in years." Dad smiled.

"I know. It's nothing. It's just this thing with Pat and me."

"Chile, what thing is this that's got you glowing? Has that boy finally seen sense and asked you out?"

Wow. I really doubted if Dad knew what we were up to, he'd be supportive. No matter what I was getting out of it.

"No, Dad. You know he doesn't like me like that." That was what I had to keep in the front of my mind. Pat wouldn't see me that way. There was no reason for him to. Even when he'd looked at me last night like I was the most beautiful woman he'd ever seen, I had to remember that I knew him. I knew what he was like and knew his type.

Last night had been amazing. It was a night I'd never imagined spending with a man like him.

I had to remember business though. Business was business.

"You young people."

"Dad, I'm thirty-four. I'm not all that young anymore." I laughed. "I'm old enough to not be classed in that category of the young who should know better."

"Not to me. You've done a lot for me, sweet girl. You've had to take over my duties, but please humor me in the ways that I can still help." He reached over and took my hand.

I smiled. "Okay. I'll do that."

"So, has he asked you out? You're all dressed up."

"We're just going to lunch." I was certain Dad must have known about all Pat got up to, and yet he still asked me if we were dating.

"Lunch? Why not dinner? I'm sure the reason why he's all over the place trying to find the perfect girl is because he thinks you aren't interested in him."

I shook my head. "Dad, you poor thing. I hope you don't really believe that."

He sighed and shrugged. "No, not really, but it's what I tell myself. Especially when I saw the papers the other week."

"Let's just say, he's of a different variety. People like him keep the world interesting. The papers wouldn't get their stories, and we'd all be bored with no scandals or hearing about rich guys doing all manner of crap to shake the place up." I chuckled.

He gave me a little smile. "Something's up with you.

You look happy, but it's like you're trying to stop the happiness from coming out."

"No, I don't think it's anything like that. I'd love to be happy." I would. Right now, I was in that in between stage where I didn't quite know what I was about because I wasn't the one controlling the situation. It was just happening, and we'd have to play it by ear.

"Chile, it makes me sad to hear you say that. A father always wants to see his little girl smile. What's worrying you? Besides me."

"Dad, please. I promise you I'll be okay. I just worry about you. I'm worried about this surgery, worried that something will happen to you because your being here has made your situation worse. It would be nice to have someone else around to support us. Not financially, just, you know, to talk to."

He nodded, and a grim expression washed over his face. "Angelica. She should be here."

God, I didn't even want to talk to him about my sister right now.

Yes, she should be here, but I'd accepted that she wasn't. I'd accepted a very long time ago that she was never going to be there for me the way a big sister should.

I'd known it that night she first left us. She and Dad had the worst argument ever. It was so horrible. I would never forget it. Her boyfriend picked her up, ready to take her away. She was only eighteen, and he was thirty-five.

Dad begged her to stay. He begged her to go to college or get a job, but she wouldn't listen. She left and never looked back. Over the years, we'd hear from her when she needed money. When we didn't have it to give, she'd get upset with us and we wouldn't hear from her.

I personally hadn't spoken to her in close to eight years. That was my choice, and I wouldn't be the one to put myself out to talk to her. I hadn't done anything wrong, and I didn't see the need to take on a guilt I shouldn't feel. I already felt disappointed and let down in the worst way. It was enough.

"It's okay, Dad. We have each other, and it's enough."

He took my hand and nodded. "We have each other."

He had me, I had him, and I had Lana and Pat.

Those two were close to me, each in their own way. There were things I would never tell Pat that I told Lana, and there were experiences I'd had with Pat that I'd never share with Lana.

No one would believe that we could be that close yet not involved.

I was having a hard time believing it myself after last night.

I guess, though, that maybe I was just stuck on the afterglow of feeling something special.

Dancing with him for hours on end, doing something completely unexpected.

Dad gave my hand a gentle squeeze. "We're going to be okay, baby girl. I know the good Lord will bless you with all good things. He always takes care of his angels."

That was a nice thing to say. I appreciated it and hoped I wasn't jumping from the frying pan into the fire.

Pat sat at one of the tables outside of the restaurant.

He was looking through a newspaper. It looked like the *L.A. Times*. He either read that or *The Chronicle*.

He didn't see me until I got close to him.

I chose a pair of shorts today with a peach camisole top. My hair was still very curly from my French roll last night, so I wore it down, hanging in glorious curls.

When he saw me, I noticed him do that thing he always did when something, or someone, piqued his interest.

It was strange having him look at me like that. I guess I really had changed somewhat from the woman I used to be back in New York. I knew I hadn't exactly become some sort of beast, but the difference when I had done myself up like last night was very striking.

"Hey." I smiled as I lowered myself into the seat in front of him.

He set the paper down, leaned forward, and took a lock of my hair, allowing the curl to swivel around his thumb.

"Hmmm," was all he said.

I didn't know if that was a hmmm as in he was thinking about something, a new way to say hello, or ... well, I didn't know what it was. It could be anything when it came to him.

"What does that mean, Pat? Am I not to your liking today?" I motioned to myself, and his gaze dropped to my cleavage and lingered there.

"Since I'm not sure how to answer that, I'll just be quiet."

"What is that supposed to mean? If I look bad, I'd like to know." I folded my arms under my breasts, and he frowned.

"Can you stop doing that?"

"Stop doing what?" I cooed, just the way I did yesterday before I took his credit card.

"And stop talking all sexy and sassy, slow motion."

I laughed, leaning forward, and gazed at him. "We're at lunch, Pat. Didn't you invite me out so we could be a show? That is what I'm doing, playing my part." I winked at him.

"Actually, I just invited you out for a normal lunch. But you're right. It's buzz."

It was buzz indeed because right over there by the water fountain, not even twenty feet away, was a man with his phone trying to get a picture of us.

He didn't even try to hide or act like he wasn't when he saw me look at him.

"Well, the paparazzi are here. God, I'm actually amazed at how much attention you get since all you do is property development. Imagine if you were a rock star or a model."

He laughed, showing off his dimples, highlighting the angles and planes of his gorgeous face. It was the answer to my comment.

He got the attention because he was gorgeous and had a history of dating celebs. Add the wealth, and he was a done deal for the *National Enquirer*.

When last I checked, his net worth was a few million. It made me feel all anxious, so I stopped looking at things like that. That was four years ago. We were still getting to know each other then. I was certain with all he'd done since then that his net worth was significantly more now.

"I'm just going to overlook that comment of yours, Georgia French." He tilted his head to the side and glanced over his shoulder at the man watching us.

It did feel awkward. More than usual. I guess I hadn't noticed the attention as much before.

"I can't believe he's just sitting there waiting for something to happen. We haven't even ordered yet." It was beyond me how people could do that.

I got embarrassed if I got caught staring at a person. These guys didn't care. It must have been one of those things where it took a certain kind of person to do certain jobs. And, just like I'd said to Dad, we'd all be bored if we weren't entertained by a little gossip and scandal every now and again.

It was just miles different if you were the object or subject of said gossip and scandal.

"Do you want to go somewhere else?" Pat's voice cut into my thoughts.

If this were last month, I would have said yes. But this right here was exactly what we wanted. Attention. We wanted attention for this plan of ours to work.

It was attention from the right people. People who could spread gossip like wildfire. It would make it all believable and add nourishment to the seeds we'd sowed last night.

It was perfect.

"No, it's actually perfect. We should give him something to... stare at."

The words came out of my mouth, but I didn't know

what to do. I hadn't planned any of this. I hadn't planned a process for what I would do if we were in a situation like this. Pat, on the other hand, looked like he had.

"Come here," he said. His eyes sparkled with mischief. Something sinful and devilishly wicked.

"What are we doing?" I leaned forward and asked.

His mouth curled up into a slow, easy smile, and he reached over and took my hand, tugging on it for me to get up.

"Just come to me."

Okay, I could do this. I could do this whole public eye thing with the billionaire playboy who drove me crazy. I could do this, whatever it was we were doing, by focusing on the vision of getting all my dreams and everything I ever wanted.

I stood up and went to him, exuding a confidence I didn't feel.

Little did I know that his aim was to pull me down into his lap.

I laughed at the ridiculousness of it. Me sitting in his lap. No one would believe I would willingly do this. No one who knew me.

"I'm in your lap." I couldn't stop laughing. "This is what you think of? Your dad is going to think this looks fake as hell, like we were just messing around." I placed my hand on his chest.

His muscles felt harder today.

He slipped his arm around me and pulled me closer. Although he was still smiling, something cunning lurked in his eyes. Something that got my attention.

It caught and held it.

"We don't look like we're messing around, Georgie," he pointed out.

"Don't we?"

"No, not one damn bit."

"What do we look like, then?"

"Like a different version of us."

I couldn't tear my gaze away from his. I stared until I got lost in the rich green hue of his eyes and I noticed for the first time that there were slight variations in the tone. Dark, then light and darker.

My nerved scattered all across my waist as he ran his fingers up to take another lock of my hair.

He looked at it like he was contemplating something. When he looked back to me, his gaze darkened and intensified.

My hands started trembling because I sensed something deep in the pit of my stomach as to what I felt like doing.

The kiss. A kiss.

Let it happen naturally...

That was what Lana had suggested. Great idea if this thing Pat and I were doing were real. Not so great if we were pretending we were real.

That was what I thought. I laughed at the idea of naturally allowing myself to know when I'd feel like kissing because I would have bet the two million I didn't have yet that it would never happen.

Yet, here I was with those deep emotions swirling within me.

The line between friendship blurred before my eyes. It was fading so fast I could barely see it.

I could tell from the look in his eyes that he felt it too.

When you'd known someone for as long as I knew him, and knew so much about them, you knew what they were thinking even without them saying it.

"Please, for the love of God, don't slap me," he whispered.

"No."

He moved his hand up to cup my chin. "Come here."

His voice, deep and low, seeped into me, and like an obedient servant, I went to him as he guided my lips to meet his.

He brushed his lips over mine for a brief intro, then moved back to press harder for an actual kiss. His lips on mine.

The moment he did, heat rushed over my entire body. It was like throwing a match on gasoline and watching it spread until it combusted.

He angled my face to deepen the kiss, and I slid my arms up the hard planes of his powerful chest.

I kissed him back with the same desire he showed me when he pushed his tongue into my mouth, and I tasted him.

God, I didn't think I'd ever craved or hungered for anything like this because when I tasted him, it was like I couldn't get enough.

He tasted like pure desire, passion, and temptation all rolled into one. He was like a blast of oxygen filling my body with something I never knew I needed.

Everything left my mind. It all left me, and I experienced a gamut of emotions fighting to break free.

This was not a mere kiss for the street.

This was not a *mere* kiss. End of story. It was something else. Something that terrified me because it was him.

Patterson Flynn.

It was that thought that made me pull away. Pull away and break the very best kiss I'd ever had in my life.

Shock registered on his face. Possibly shock from the way we'd kissed and from me backing away.

The cameras were all going now. I looked around and saw them. It wasn't just the man by the water fountain.

"I just remembered... I have a thing I have to do," I stuttered and slid off his lap.

"Georgie... I..."

Yes, he was shocked too. I could tell.

"I, um... I'll call you later."

I rushed away before he could say his next words.

Pretend...

I didn't think I was pretending anymore.

That kiss was real.

The kiss was real, but I had to remember that none of this whole drama was.

Pat and I were not real.

Forgetting that would be a very, very big mistake.

CHAPTER 14

Patterson

LAST NIGHT...

Dancing with her last night had been like nothing I could describe.

I was trying really hard to keep the focus. Keep the focus of the mission I was trying to pull off.

It faded away the minute I had seen Georgie walk down those stairs at the club and into my arms for the night.

Then the kiss...

Fuck.

I wished someone had told me it was going to feel

like that. I wished I'd known ahead of time that kissing her was going to make me feel like I was walking on air with fire covering my body. A weird concoction of an image, but that was the best way I could describe it.

That was how I felt as I left the restaurant and headed straight to the one person I could always talk to.

Ivan.

He was in the garage working on one of his motorcycles. It was the Kawasaki. I borrowed that one the most and probably used it more than him. Realistically, I should have bought the damn thing from him, but I knew how much he loved it.

I could have bought my own, but I liked borrowing his cars and bikes. It gave us something to do.

Sometimes it was an excuse to see him these days because he was so loved up with his wife that I barely saw him like I used to.

He chuckled when he saw me coming.

"Duuude, I was just thinking about you. I got a new part for the Harley, and it rides like a dream. I got new tires too." Ivan beamed. He stood up and smiled at me.

There was grease on his cheeks and on his forehead.

"That sounds good."

"You alright? You look like… well. You look like you've seen a ghost."

It was sort of how I felt too inside. That realization that something you didn't think was real was real. So, sure, he was spot on with that because when I'd first thought of kissing Georgie, I thought the setting was perfect.

I just didn't know I was going to feel the way I did after. Like I never wanted to stop kissing her, and like I wanted more.

"In a manner of speaking." I cracked my knuckles. "Are you and Jada busy?"

"No, she's baking cookies inside, but that's it. We're doing something for charity. I was going to call you later. I have something to tell you." He looked like he had really good news.

"Oh, tell me now."

"Well, how about you tell me what's going on with you first? You look like you need to talk," he observed.

I stared at the guy I'd been friends with forever. He was more of a brother to me.

The brother I'd never had. We were both only children in our families, so we took each other for siblings. All this time, all these long years, and I was always the one who took up the time to talk about my problems first. I was the one who always got us in a mess when we were two crazy high school boys trying to figure out how much more trouble we could get in.

He always took the road of logic, then had to make a U-turn to get me and pull me out of shit I got myself into.

Today, I didn't want to be selfish. I wanted to hear his news first.

"You go first. It sounds like amazing news." I nodded.

His face lit up when I said that, and he smiled. "It is. It's really amazing, actually. Jada's pregnant. I'm going to be a father."

I smiled, feeling his excitement the longer he looked at me. "My God. That is amazing."

Feeling overwhelmed with the joy from the news, I hugged him, completely ecstatic.

He hugged me back and laughed. "Wow, I'm loving this reaction. I thought you would be the one person to whine at me and point out how much more my life's going to change."

He stepped back and looked at me.

"No, I'm happy for the two of you. Congratulations, you deserve happiness. I just can't believe you're going to be a father."

And I was here to talk about a kiss.

A kiss. Like we were back in our freshman year of high school and planning which girls we were going to kiss before the school year was out.

Fucking hell. I hated to point this out, but Dad was right. He'd said I wasn't even behaving like a twenty-six-year-old looking for a good opportunity.

Today, I didn't even feel like that. I was more comparable to a sixteen-year-old.

The front door of the house opened, and Jada came out carrying a tray of cookies.

The smile on her face was as bright as the sunshine.

She reminded me a lot of my Georgie. Same dark skin, same vibrancy, similar hairstyles. Jada was a little more extravagant and sassier. But then, so had my Georgie been over the last few days.

My Georgie.

I'd called her that for so long it seemed to take place as part of my vocabulary and mind. But thinking it now felt different to me.

Jada practically skipped toward us.

"Hey, I saw you pull up. Did he tell you?" she bubbled, setting the cookie tray down on the table to give me a quick hug.

"Yes. I heard you'll be the newest yummy mommy on the block. Congratulations," I answered.

I didn't think it was possible, but her face brightened even more. "Thanks so much. We just can't believe it."

"I can." This was the part where I would have usually said something crazy like what would they expect with the amount of time they spent in the bedroom and devouring each other.

That wasn't me today though. This was special. It

was good news that looked like it brought them even closer. They hadn't even been together a year yet, and look at them. Married with a baby on the way, and they looked so much in love.

Ivan put his arm around her and pulled her in for a hug and a kiss.

"Stay for dinner, buddy." Ivan nodded.

"I'll make lasagna," Jada added. "With those fiery chilis you like."

"I'd like that. Thank you."

"I'll leave you boys to talk." Jada chuckled. "Come in when you're ready. I'll make some more stuff."

"Goddess, don't work too much. I don't want you on your feet for too long," Ivan said.

He still called her goddess, even now. First, he'd made a joke of it, then it stuck.

"I won't." One more kiss before she sauntered away, back into the house.

"Okay, what's up? You have a weird look about you, and it's rattling me." Ivan grinned. He leaned back against his worktable and folded his arms.

I looked at him and wondered how to start this conversation.

"I kissed Georgie," I began. Best to get it out and off my chest. Quick and fast like ripping off a Band-Aid.

"Okay, was it like you planned? With all the people to see you?"

We'd been talking the other day. I mentioned a kiss in public. But I couldn't come up with a plan on how I'd actually do it.

It didn't feel like something I could plan. Not with her.

Now I knew why.

"People were there, yes, but that wasn't the problem."

He tilted his head to the side and quirked a brow. "There was a problem?"

"Yes... no... yes." I winced.

"Which is it?"

I frowned and ran my hand through my hair. "Ivan, this feels like immature shit. You just told me you're having a baby, and I'm talking like we're boys back in high school."

He smiled. "It's different stages of a relationship, man. That's all it is. You know, though, at least back in high school you used to listen to me. Not a lot, but more often than not."

"What do you mean?"

"Let's rewind a little bit. You didn't say why the kiss was a problem. According to the plan, you wanted to create this public buzz so it would seem more believable to your father that you two got engaged. Kissing her in public was the best thing you could have done that because I can bet my ass it'll be in the papers tomorrow. So, what's the problem, man?" The way he looked… he knew. He knew what the problem was but wanted me to say it.

It was like teaching a child a lesson they'd already been cautioned about, except that this lesson wasn't something anyone had taught me. I'd learned it for myself.

I felt it for myself.

"The kiss was real," I confessed.

"Oh, *really?*" Sarcasm was all over his face. He even chuckled.

"Yes. The damn kiss was real, and the date last night was real too. Ivan, you should have seen her. I danced with her the whole night to those old jazz songs my grandparents used to dance to, and I never wanted to stop. Then, when I kissed her today, I never wanted to stop that either, but we did, and I remembered this shit I brewed up myself."

There it was, all my feelings. Everything I felt and the epiphany that dawned on me.

The epiphany that dawned on me after only a few days.

He raised both brows now.

"Patterson, didn't you think it was weird that I never brought her name up as we tried to brainstorm girl-friends of the past and women in your life?"

I nodded. "Of course, I thought it was weird. Why didn't you?"

"It was because I guess I'm a little protective of her. She may not have realized it, but it was always real for her."

I narrowed my eyes at him. "What are you saying?"

"I'm a relationship psychotherapist, man. If I can't spot those types of signs, then I'm not much use, am I? I never mentioned her because I could see that she had real feelings for you, and I knew this would get messy when you realized you had feelings for her too. It helped that you promised her there would be no one else because it made you put your focus on the woman who's been in front of you this whole time. People don't behave the way you guys do as friends. You're like an old married couple. I thought it was better for you to see what would happen with someone else because I was against the fact that you'd been told to find a woman to marry from day one. I didn't like that, and I thought she deserved more than being with you so you could get the Flynn empire."

I couldn't have felt like more of an asshole. "What do I do now? Ivan, there's no way in hell she'd want to be with a guy like me. Knowing and seeing all I've done, and now this."

"Well, you two agreed to this plan, and it's in motion now. I can't tell you what to do about it. I understand where your old man's coming from, but damn. What I can advise you on is this, if you want the girl, go after the girl. Forget the details of everything else. Man up and earn her respect. I know Georgie knows all manners of shit even I don't know. I guess it's a good thing, though, that she stuck around. And, for fuck's sake, two million is a lot of money, but we both know she's not all about the money. There might be something in there she's not telling you. But one step at a time."

"One step at a time," I repeated. This felt like I'd be taking giant steps.

He nodded and smiled. "One step at a time, man."

Okay. I could do this.

I wanted the girl. I wanted her bad. She was like temptation waving itself in front of me.

She wouldn't, however, be as easy to get like the others. She knew me, which was my downfall. But I'd do it.

I wanted her too much to fail.

Act now and work out the kinks later.

CHAPTER 15

Georgie

LANA BROUGHT out a tray of sandwiches and sweet tea.

Lunch.

Lunch I should have been having with Pat.

I didn't tell her what happened. Not yet. I was still trying to figure out how to tell her I practically ran away from Pat after kissing him.

It was ridiculous.

She knew something was up with me though because we hadn't planned on seeing each other today. I was also abnormally quiet.

We'd gone to her living room, switched on the TV

to watch the season finale of *The Real Housewives of Atlanta,* and hadn't really spoken. I'd noticed her observe me though, as the show played.

She'd then gone to make the food.

She set the tray down on the coffee table and switched off the TV in the middle of an infomercial for weed killer.

She sat opposite me and crossed her legs one over the other as she glared at me.

"So, did you sleep with him?" she blurted. "I'm trying to figure out if that's what it is, but I'm not sure. I think if you did, you would have come by earlier. This is late for you, and a little too impromptu for it to be about that. So, I'm not sure."

Truth be told, if I'd slept with him, my behavior would have been more understandable.

It was time to spill the tea and tell her how I was feeling.

"I didn't sleep with him," I confessed.

"So, what happened, then? Something happened between you two. I can see it. It's all over you. Clear as day." She pointed one perfectly manicured finger at me.

I gazed at her, suddenly feeling more appreciative of the friendship we had. "We kissed. It was just a kiss. You know how you said to let it happen naturally? It did." Boy, did it ever.

"It did, and it was real?" She pursed her pink lips together.

"Yeah. It was damn real. It was real, and I practically fled. Lana... this just went a way I never expected."

"I told you, you liked him."

That was basically the equivalent of hearing her say 'I told you so.'

"You also told me I'd like deep fried pig's nuts too, and I wouldn't even try it." She laughed at that. Me too, from the memory. That was back in high school.

"Girl, I didn't even know what the hell I was eating. It was that weird girl from the carnival who gave it to me."

"Whatever, the fact that it was called pig's nuts and smelled like shit was a dead giveaway." The laughter helped ease my mind.

"Okay, we've established that pig's nuts are pig's nuts. The same as we established that Georgia French likes Patterson Flynn a whole lot more than she thought she would. Or did."

I brought my hand to my head, not wanting to believe it. It was very true though. No point denying it or lying to myself.

"He's absolutely wrong for me." I was reiterating that to myself.

"We can say that about a lot of guys, Georgie. I speak from experience. And we say it for different

BELLA FONTAINE & KHARDINE GRAY

reasons. Sometimes, though, the guys you think are wrong for you are actually the ones who interest us and can surprise us in more ways than one."

I sighed. She was echoing the words from my heart. Last night had been magical. "Why are you always so insightful and right?"

"I know more than I get credit for. I also, on occasion, don't hold a grudge. People do what they have to sometimes. We just have to accept that everyone is different."

I felt the emotion behind her words. She really was speaking from experience. The O'Shea family, whom she grew up with, had a son a year older than her. His name was Ryan. He was the high school bully. They had a secret relationship and planned to run off together after her mother died, but it didn't work out. She always used to talk about how wrong he was for her. But then he turned out to be the guy who captured her heart.

The message behind her words was that people could surprise you. I understood that completely. I just didn't know if I could apply the concept to myself.

Doing so would mean forgetting all the craziness I'd seen Pat get up to. That was going to be very hard.

"I'm not sure I can forget all I've seen Pat do, Lana." I shook my head.

"I'm not asking you to do that. I know you though. I

know you must have thought about him this way. Also, you haven't told me about last night. How did it go?"

My heart melted. I sighed and filled her in on all the details, gushing and drooling over him like I was sixteen years old and back in high school.

"Oh my God. I can't believe you're talking about the same guy. He danced with you? *To jazz?*"

I nodded. "Yeah. He did."

"So, this kiss. Was it in public?" She added, "For all to see?"

"Yes. It was a very public kiss."

"Great, so mission accomplished. Time to move it along to phase two."

"Phase two?"

"Yes. People already assumed you're doing the dirty with your boss. Now they know for damn sure if they got pictures of the two of you kissing in public." She nodded, and I could see a plan brewing in her mind.

"It feels like a mess, Lana."

"It doesn't have to be. The show's already in motion. All you guys have to do is control what happens next."

"What if it wasn't real for him? Why would it be?" This wasn't like I was talking about someone I'd just met.

"Only you can answer that. You must have known if he was faking it or not."

I wished I believed he was faking it. I really did. It

would be easier to believe he was the guy I was used to rather than to think of this new version of him I'd suddenly met.

"Well... let's just say it was real. I know what he's like, Lana. I know him. I know what he's like with women. I can't allow myself to be treated like that. To be used and treated like a hookup. I can't be that woman. I can't just... sweep all that stuff under the rug either. And look at this stupid plan I got myself mixed up in. It's just like him to think up something fake rather than work for the real thing." My head... it actually felt like it was going to explode.

"Girl, you are going at a hundred miles an hour. I love the foresight and the hindsight, but both of those aren't always good things. Life is for living. If you're always contemplating possibilities, you'll never do anything spontaneously or take a risk on something crazy that may pan out."

She got my attention. That was me. Always planning for the future or thinking about the past. Thinking up ways I could change it all. I didn't believe in adding more problems to my plate. Plus, there was the looming possibility of me starting up my business, which meant leaving him. It wasn't really that big of a deal, but I knew he'd take a hit because I did so much for him.

"There's so much to think about."

"In the grand scheme of things yes, there is. But I'm

trying to get you to push the bigger picture out of the way and open the door for something else. Something lighthearted and fun. I get that you don't want to get involved like that, but let's look at this a little deeper. You knew full well what the man was like, but you have continued to work for him all these long years. You also knew what you were getting into with this fake relationship. Working things to your advantage isn't a bad thing."

"Isn't it?"

"Did you enjoy the kiss?" She intensified her stare.

"Yes."

"Did you want more than just the kiss?"

I frowned. "Yeah. I shouldn't though—"

"So, if there was more, you wouldn't take it?" She interrupted and gave me an incredulous look.

What a question.

"I don't know. I shouldn't—"

"Georgie, stop right there," she interrupted again. "Since you appear to have lost your zing and common sense, I'm going to tell you, if there is more, take it. You hear me? You take it. Take the damn man if you get the chance. Please, for the love of God, don't shriek away or think of logic. Ride this thing out and see what happens next. There's a thing called having fun. You can do that. You're allowed to have fun with a gorgeous man. No matter who he is. Just relax and let it happen naturally."

I smirked. Could it really be that easy?

"*Naturally?* Lana, I don't know how many more natural things I can take."

"Just remember safe sex, or if you're taking the pill, stock up. All that pent-up desire is bound to unleash." She laughed.

"Oh my God, Lana," I chided, but I couldn't stop my mind from drifting down that path.

"Georgie, the next time you come running to me better be because you had too much sex."

We both laughed, but when the laughter faded, I wondered if I could be so chilled and have fun.

Lana was like that. She could be that way with a guy and be fine with it.

To me, Pat wasn't any old guy.

We only kissed today, and look how I reacted.

What if we found ourselves in a situation where there would be more?

Could I just have fun with him?

Lana had never given me advice that didn't pan out one way or another.

I just wasn't sure how I'd be. What I'd do.

I knew Pat. She didn't know him the way I did.

This was all so far out of my comfort zone. I didn't know what the hell I was doing, and the fact that from one day to the next things could change like the wind was so unpredictable.

That kiss though…

Oh Lord…

Okay. Maybe I really could roll with the natural and see what happened.

I seriously hoped it didn't blow up in my face.

I couldn't take any more disappointment. I was fragile from all I'd been through, and my heart was the only thing I had left.

The only strength. It still clung to my dreams.

I couldn't allow it to break.

That would break me too.

CHAPTER 16

Patterson

Patterson Flynn's New Toy. How long will she last?

That was the headline in today's *Chronicle.*

Then there was a big old picture of me kissing Georgie at the restaurant, and under that was one of us at the club on Friday.

We were news. Front-page-worthy news, as if there weren't more important things going on in L.A. and the world at large.

Like most people, I hated Mondays and loathed Monday mornings. Today carried with it a tension I didn't need. Two weeks ago brought with it a change to my life that I never saw coming with this whole new problem Dad had laid down on me.

Today showed the fruits of my labor, and instead of being happy to see that we had the media exactly where we wanted them, I felt torn by some of the things they said.

I knew Georgie hated attention like this, and they made her out to be this week's woman. Like I'd get rid of her by the weekend.

She wasn't in her office when I'd come in today. I got here earlier just to talk to her. I would have called last night or even Saturday, but I'd held back on it. Better to talk to her in person.

A knock on my door took my attention away from the contracts I was signing. It turned out I had thirty new businesses to work with. That meant thirty different sets of paperwork to look through before the contracts were signed off by me and we started working with them.

"Come in," I called out.

It was Dad. I was sort of hoping it would be Georgie, but she didn't usually knock.

He came in with a tentative smile on his face and stopped just in front of my desk.

"Morning, son."

"Morning. You okay?" It was unusual for him to come and see me first thing on a Monday.

"Yeah, I'm okay. I just came to see how you were."
He looked at the newspaper on my desk, then back to
me as I leaned back in my chair. "The papers are very
interesting this morning. I was wondering too if there
was something you had to tell me. Anything out of the
ordinary between you and Georgie I should know
about? Anything, *different*, between you two."

"No, not really." I was completely messing with him.
He knew it too.

"Patterson, do I have to drag it out of you? I can see
the picture of you two right in front of me." He pointed
at it and smirked. "You kiss your PA like that on the
regular?"

"Nope, just on Saturdays and before two on
Sundays." I chuckled. I was joking around, but it really
was best to be subtle about this for more reasons
than one.

"Fine, whatever, be difficult. I'll just say you two
look good together." He nodded. "She's a great girl. I
always liked her. It would be nice if my proposal has
shifted your sights to what may be right in front of you.
It would be nice too if it made you calm down some to
open your mind."

I stared at him, listening to what he was saying.
Really listening. He didn't seem as demanding as he had
been two weeks ago. This was more of a fatherly chat
of encouragement.

"Thank you. I'll consider it. I'll consider her. We do seem to be getting on really well. I like her. Looks like I seem to like her more than I imagined. Who knows what can happen in the next few weeks?"

"Well, if you need to talk, I'm all ears." He gave me that tentative look again. "I saw her in the garden, sitting on the bench near the fountain. She was by herself doing paperwork. Didn't know if that was her new thing or if she needed to get away from the office for fresh air. Hope she's okay."

He was right to mention that because Georgie didn't do that. Monday morning saw her here in the office with me, planning for the day. Her being in the garden at this hour was absolute evidence that she probably wasn't okay.

"Thanks, I'd better go check on her."

He smiled at that answer and left.

I made my way down to the garden two minutes later. I walked around the row of roses into the section with the lilies. That was where I found her, exactly where Dad had said. Sitting on the bench.

She wore a powder-pink camisole top. Her hair was pulled back into a ponytail that showed off her high cheekbones. The ends tapered into one big curl that flowed down her back and picked up in the winds as it drifted through the flowers.

She looked beautiful. Beautiful like a vision of pure

perfection. Beautiful like she'd just stepped away from the heavenly hosts of angels.

Beautiful and perfect, and I couldn't believe I'd known this perfect being for over five years and was only just noticing that.

What the hell was wrong with me?

I stopped to watch her, just for a few seconds. I wanted to look at her just like this. Outside, in her element, without any influences or stresses from me.

She was writing in a little notebook. Next to her was a foolscap folder that held a few documents. On top of the folder was a copy of *The Chronicle*. She would have seen today's story.

Seeing that, I decided to continue my path to her. I was interested to know what she was thinking after reading the papers.

She didn't see me until I was paces away, and when she looked up, I noticed the shimmer of gold she'd used to highlight her cheekbones. It glittered in the sun and created the focus and attention it was made to create.

She gave me a little smile, but I could see caution in her eyes.

I didn't want her to be cautious or wary around me. I wanted her to be Georgie. My Georgie.

I walked over to her and sat beside her on the bench.

She shuffled around to look at me.

"Come here often?" I asked and grinned.

She smiled at me. "When I need to think or get away, I come here. It was, um … just the attention in the office. People read the papers and were asking me stuff. I came out here to do some work."

"I'm sorry. You don't like having attention on you like this, and you're in the middle of it in the worst way," I pointed out. My gaze dropped to her lips, and memories of that kiss came flooding back.

Memories of how my blood had heated up and danced through my veins. Memories of how much more I wanted, and how I wanted her.

"I knew what I was getting into. I guess, though, that I never expected the papers to be so mean. *New toy...* I suppose your old toys didn't mind being called toys as long as they were with you."

Shit, I knew it bothered her. There was always something to draw the focus to any negativity about me in some form.

The thing was, up until last week, I didn't think that was negative. If this had happened to one of the women I usually hooked up with, I would have thought nothing of it.

I would have been more like... Well, honestly, I wouldn't care.

This was Georgie though, and Ivan's words kept ringing through my mind. Singing to me and telling me that I needed to man up.

"You're not a toy. You aren't a toy to me. You never were and wouldn't be even without this plan of ours. *Mine*. My plan."

She laughed. "Pat, if not for your plan, *our* plan, I wouldn't ever know what it feels like to be part of the toy box."

It was just like her to joke around like that.

"Georgie, I'm serious."

"Okay, Pat, let's take the plan out of the equation. What do you think would have happened to us?"

I had to look away from her because I knew we would have continued the same as we had been for the next ten years. However, just because I felt that might have happened didn't mean it was set in stone.

It was just one possibility, so there could have been any number of possibilities. I could pick one.

I looked back to her and smiled. "It would happen like this... We're playing *Call of Duty* or something, we're eating pizza, and you take a break to go grab us some drinks. Suddenly, I notice you're wearing those yoga pants that make your legs look sexy, and then I can't stop myself. I have to fulfill the overwhelming urge to kiss you, so I do, and you slap me because you think I'm possessed by the devil. But then you come to your senses when you realize I'm not possessed and kiss me too."

She was right about her assessment that I was crazy.

That was some kind of crazy, but it worked. She burst out laughing, and it was the best sound ever. It made me want to think up all kinds of shit to tell her so she wouldn't stop.

This moment wasn't about that.

It was something else. Something I knew deep down in my heart but was afraid of. I'd never met or been with a woman who made me want to see more of her, or get to know more about her.

I'd never imagined meeting one who would work that kind of magic on me. I didn't know any existed who could unlock this thing in me that made me want to try, and here I was sitting next to her. Not even thinking about the Flynn empire.

How could that be?

So, laughing was great, but this was me doing something different to see what would happen. I was by no means suitable to begin to climb up the scale of the kind of guy I saw her with, but I was going to try my luck.

"You are so crazy." She giggled. "It's a nice story though. I love that you assume I'd come to my senses and conclude you weren't possessed and kiss you back."

"Of course, why wouldn't you?"

She smiled. "Well, there's no one watching. No papers around to capture the moment. No one to see you kiss me because—"

I had to stop her. I moved to her lips and stopped her with a kiss. I pressed my lips to hers and reached for her beautiful face. Guiding her to me, wanting her to stay there. I kissed her gently, her soft, sweet lips, loving the taste of her. Wanting more.

I stopped and moved back, only inches away, and gazed into those beautiful eyes of hers.

"Because I wanted to. There's no one to see me kiss you because I want to. There doesn't need to be anyone." I ran my finger along the underside of her jaw, smiling as I caressed the smooth, silky skin there while she looked stunned. "In my vision, there was just us at my place. But today we're here in the garden. Just us. Here's the part where you can slap me first then kiss me, but you can just kiss me if you want since you know I'm not possessed."

She smiled at that and leaned forward, reaching for my tie to pull me closer.

As my lips touched hers again, I captured her mouth the way I wanted to and kissed her with all the desire that surged through me.

CHAPTER 17

Patterson

I HADN'T MADE out like that since high school.

We sat there for a good two hours just kissing. I couldn't bring myself to stop kissing her, and I didn't want to leave. What broke us apart was the gardener coming through the little gate behind us.

That was the only thing that was able to force reality back into our minds.

I wasn't even thinking about work. In my head I was done for the day and ready to continue my indulgence in her, but I allowed her to leave because she had some meeting with her father and his doctor.

I had to wait until the next day to see her, and it didn't help that we had a damn meeting first thing in the morning with a bunch of people who hated my guts.

The host of investors with ninety percent of them casting daggers my way and Hudson with his black eye.

Dad, Georgie, Dad's secretary, Mirabel, and the ten percent of investors who didn't really allow my actions to bother them were the only people who I bothered to acknowledge.

The room consisted of twelve of us.

Georgie sat next to Mirabel, two seats away from me, taking minutes as Dad talked about the forecast for the next three months. Everything was looking good for us.

More clients, more money, a new vision, new ideas, lots in the works to take us through the year and right into the next.

He spoke with enthusiasm, and I was sure what he was saying was all good stuff, but I didn't really hear the bulk of it.

I was too busy looking at my gorgeous PA.

Fucking hell... I was completely absorbed, and it was like she made it some new mission to tempt me with her body.

Today, she wore red, which looked just as good on her as pink and every other color known to man.

The red top she wore clung to her body, making a great show of her perfect breasts.

It was one of those empire-line tops that I believed were designed by the devil to lure men into temptation. That fucking dog Hudson tried to look at her too, but he caught me watching him, and I made sure the look on my face told him I'd really mess him up this time if I got my hands on him.

She was mine to look at. I was the single one here, not him, and if I really wanted to cause trouble, I would have called his wife and told her exactly what her husband got up to on these business trips.

I had a strong feeling she knew though. He was too blasé about it for her not to know. He acted like he didn't care who knew, or if she knew.

I didn't waste too much time on him. One look was enough to fend him off.

I would admit, though, that he was the reason why I was still sitting here.

The way I felt now, with my cock practically fighting to break out of my pants, I would have taken Georgie and left this meeting within the first five minutes when Dad informed us on how well we were doing as a company. For me that said job done, tick the box.

With Hudson here, I had to show I was serious. Even with my lust-filled mind, I had to show the people in here that I was serious about my leadership of the company. I couldn't act like the playboy today.

Or at least for the next fifteen minutes.

We'd been in here for an hour already. It was an hour of me sitting here watching Georgie and half listening to Dad.

Dad cleared his throat in an exaggerated way that I knew from my thirty-six years of experience was aimed at me.

I snapped my gaze to him only to suddenly find everyone looking at me.

He must have said something or asked me something I didn't hear. Again.

I wasn't sure if it was a yes or no question, or what the hell he'd said.

Dad raised his brows, but I didn't miss the slight humor in his expression, which suggested he'd seen me looking at Georgie.

"I'm sorry, can you repeat what you said? I want to be sure I cover everything." Damn, I didn't know if that was a nice save or not.

At least I sounded intelligent on some level. Not like some hormone-crazed teenager.

"Certainly. I wanted to know what you thought about the prospects of the Miami Beach project." Dad smiled.

Thank God it was that. I couldn't answer much about anything else.

"I think it will take us into the next phase of success." I pulled in a deep breath and relaxed my shoulders. "It'll be the kind of place that people look forward to opening up because of what it's been like over the last decade. Miami Beach is beautiful. We're just going to add to the beauty."

Now, that answer was stellar. Dad looked proud. That was all I needed. It didn't matter what anyone else thought.

He continued talking and guided everyone's attention to the next slide of his presentation from the overhead projector that presented the estimates figures we'd drawn up with the team.

I diverted my attention back to Georgie.

She'd shuffled, and the top moved slightly so I could see more of the swells of her breasts. It must have been the intensity of my stare and the uncontrollable desire I felt, because she looked to me and her cheeks flushed slightly.

Then, fuck, what I noticed next meant there was no way on earth I was allowing her to leave me today. Not for anything or anyone. I'd personally apologize to her father if he needed her, because she was mine today.

That top of hers showed off more than her beauty. It told me she wanted me too.

Against the fabric, I watched her nipples pressing, hardening to two points as if she was cold.

I thanked all the heavenly hosts of angels when Dad said, "Well, that's it for today. Any questions?"

Screw manners and pleasantries. I wasn't staying for questions and the shit they usually talked about after meetings.

I stood up and bowed my head curtly. "I have to rush to another meeting with my PA. Great to see you all."

That was all they were going to get out of me.

I grabbed Georgie's hand and ushered her through the door, not giving a shit who was watching us.

"Pat, what are you doing?" she protested.

I pulled her along the corridor aiming for the janitor's closet. I figured I could make it there.

"Getting privacy."

"Pat, we have contracts to go through. The prep school in Malibu got their planning permission revoked, and the church downtown wants to meet with you about refurbishing within the building protection they have to follow." It must have been nerves because she said all that in a babble.

Damn it, the janitor's closet didn't just have the one janitor inside it, but three. Three guys were inside going through the cleaning supplies. It looked like they were doing an audit.

I frowned and stopped with her.

"Pat." She giggled. "Why are you taking me to the janitor's closet?"

I didn't know how she could ask me that. I whirled around to face her and grimaced.

"Baby, look at my dick." That was the first thing that came out of my mouth. We both looked down at the distinct bulge against my pants. "You and your top have me pitching a fucking tent."

It was so bad I whipped off my jacket and kept it in front of me.

She was trying not to laugh but failed. "My top didn't do anything to you."

I'd rip that right off her first.

I grabbed the end of it and tugged, bunching it up so more of her breasts showed.

"You can blame it for what happens next." I knew where we could go.

Back to my office. Put the 'Do not disturb' sign up and lock the damn door.

I smiled wide at the wild thought of her bent over my desk.

"What happens next?"

"Come, let's go." I tugged on her hand and led her right back there. It was on the other side of the building. Too far away for me.

Too far away for all I wanted to do to her.

The sign was the first thing I put up.

When we got inside, I locked the door and diverted all calls to hell. I pressed 'Divert' without giving them a destination and didn't care where they went.

Then I grabbed her, picked her up, and set her on top of my desk.

She didn't protest when I captured her mouth to kiss her, and not when I filled my palms with her gorgeous breasts, squeezing and kneading, enjoying her moan into our kiss.

Her lips tasted amazing, but I was eager to taste the rest of her.

Tracing kisses down her neck, I moved down to her right breast and sucked the little nipple through that red silky fabric.

This was me wanting all of her, me wanting to enjoy her perfection, and I was damn straight going to enjoy her. Once I could tear myself away, I lifted the top over her head along with her bra, feeling my mouth water when her breasts spilled out and bobbled invitingly toward me, the caramel-dipped nipples begging to be sucked.

"Georgia, you're fucking perfect. I want you."

I didn't even realize I was calling her by her full name. I'd done that the other day too. She looked at me watching her, her full red lips parted, those sultry eyes looking at me like she wanted me as badly as I wanted her.

"Then take me, Patterson Flynn."

"With pleasure."

CHAPTER 18

Georgie

My God...

This was actually happening.

In Pat's office...

Me, in Pat's office, sitting here topless on top of his desk while he kissed me.

As far as I knew, he'd never done this with anyone before.

It was my one thing to claim with him. He'd never had women in his office like this.

He told me that was a big no, no. So, me being here

right now, sitting here while he feasted on me was unreal.

With that wicked smile, the godlike man trailed a line of fiery kisses all the way back down to my breasts, then nuzzled his face in the deep valley between them.

I rested my hands behind me, spread out to either side to get a good grip, giving him access to me. He took my right nipple in and sucked hard while he rubbed his thumb over the painfully hard nipple of my left breast.

I was already wet, and this made me wetter with the desire that pulled between my thighs.

I moaned into each suck, enjoying his wild suckle.

He looked like he was tasting some delicious, exotic meal he couldn't get enough of.

To have him look at me and enjoy me like that was like nothing I could quite describe.

"You're so perfect. I want all of you, all at once, baby." He smiled and took a good handful of my breasts, squeezing then kneading.

His hands felt like magic on me.

"Do I get you too?" I giggled because here I was, topless, with my skirt around my hips, while he was still fully clothed.

"Oh yes. Take whatever you want." That was like an invite to a delicious, delicious treat.

I hopped off the desk and pulled his shirt from his waistband.

There was one fantasy I'd had once. It was a dream that I quickly made myself forget and would never admit to, not even under oath, because of what it spelled out for me.

It was this, me unbuttoning his shirt, backing it down his wide, powerful shoulders so I could see the masterpiece of his perfect torso, then doing this...

I leaned forward and planted my lips against the seriously tight skin under his right pec, then I licked over it.

"Fucking hell, do that again." He shrugged off his shirt and tossed it over by my top.

I licked him again, and he groaned, pressing the hardness of his erection into my abdomen.

He took my hand and pressed it to his cock. Through his pants it felt massive. Looking down at the bulge showed what awaited me, and I yearned to have him inside me.

"This is what you do to me." He closed my fingers over his cock and moved my hand up and down the length.

"Me?"

"Yes, you sweet, delicious Georgia." He increased the pace.

I grew wet from doing just that, and he groaned deeper when I rubbed harder.

I couldn't stand it. I wanted to see him and taste him too. I undid his belt buckle, and the green of his eyes darkened when he realized what I meant to do to him.

We both watched his pants drift down his legs, then I didn't know where my bravado came from, but it came. It was all there. Oh yes, it was.

Fun...

Just like Lana had reminded me. There was a thing called fun, and I was introducing myself to wild sexual fun with Patterson Flynn, the man who'd mystified me and driven me crazy in one way or another for years.

Now, he was doing it all over again. Driving me insane with just the way he looked at me.

I pulled on the waistband of his boxers and pushed it down the taper of his hips, unleashing his massive cock that jutted free toward me like he belonged to me.

He did. Today, he was all mine.

All mine for the taking, and I couldn't believe I hadn't known how badly I wanted him until today.

He watched me with a half pain-, half pleasure-filled expression when I ran my fingers over his long length. I smiled as I lowered to my knees, and he gazed down at me like he couldn't believe what I was doing.

Taking his cock into my mouth, I licked the tip first

and enjoyed the deep groan that resonated from his chest.

It was like a triumph for me. Me, the little PA who had to take a back seat on life and watch it pass her by. Me, who'd watched him for years wondering what it would be like to be with him.

Yes...

I would admit it wholeheartedly now. I could do it. I could do it effortlessly because I knew the result of a wild fantasy that would never happen was this. This moment between us we shouldn't be having at work. This moment between my so-called boss and me that should have been forbidden. This moment between us that seemed like it was a long time coming.

It blurred the line of whatever we'd separated right out of existence.

I sucked and licked, taking him deep into my mouth, savoring the taste of him, savoring him in my hands as his cock grew in my mouth.

I licked and swallowed the pre-cum that seeped from the head of his cock and relished the salty taste.

He tugged on my arm at that moment, helping me stand.

"I need you now. I want to finish inside you, baby. Let me finish inside you."

He didn't have to ask. I wanted him just as badly as he showed me he wanted me.

"Yes," I breathed.

He kicked off his boxers and grabbed his pants again to retrieve a condom from the back pocket.

I watched him tear open the packet then roll the latex down the length of his shaft from the tip to the base.

When he reached for me, my skin heated right up at the possessiveness in his touch, and my body ached for him.

He moved me over to the floor-to-ceiling window and pressed me up against it, my back pressed to the smooth glass. His hands on either side of me.

"No one can see in, but we can see out. We can pretend they're all watching me make you mine." In all the time I'd known him, I'd never heard him speak so strongly and meaningful about anything, or anyone.

"Yours?" It sounded like something I wanted more than anything. More than anything I'd ever desired.

"Mine." He gave me a chaste kiss on my cheek that was so striking against the truly erotic sight of us. Me topless with my skirt around my waist. Him naked pressed up against me. He bent down lower to trail that kiss over to my ear and whispered, "My girl. My Georgie. My Georgia."

He then held my gaze and stared down at me like he was looking straight inside my soul.

The wicked smile returned to his face, and he

BELLA FONTAINE & KHARDINE GRAY

flipped me around to face the glass. I could see every-thing. All the people down below us walking about the office grounds, heading out to their daily lives. Some with coffee in their hands. Some with food.

It was a stage set for all to see us in the public eye, but yet this was just us.

No one knew what we were doing except us.

He ran his hand down the length of my back and pulled down my skirt and my panties, taking them all the way down my legs.

"Heels stay on, baby." He chuckled.

I turned to look behind me, but his hot hands taking hold of my hips again paralyzed me.

A second later, he pushed his finger into my core and moved in and out. Slowly then faster, then with two fingers.

Fuck... I could barely stand. He chuckled when I moaned on the wave of pleasure.

"You like that, baby?" he asked.

"Yes."

"You will like this more," he promised, and I believed him the instant he replaced his fingers with the hot head of his cock.

He thrust inside me hard and deep. So deep my knees buckled and he had to hold me up so I wouldn't fall over.

"Pat..." I groaned.

"Stay with me, baby," he said into my ear, one hand around my waist, the other secured to my hips as he started moving inside me.

Moving inside me. We were actually doing this. He was actually doing this to me.

This was us. Him and me.

Me and him.

Once I stretched to take his length, he started moving faster. Faster until we built up a great rhythm that took us. A rhythm that possessed us, and I enjoyed the hard, even strokes as he pounded into me.

And so much more when he sped up and started rutting into me. Fucking me so hard the sounds of our sweat-slicked bodies echoed in the room along with the wild sounds of us.

Then it happened. I could feel the buildup and tried so hard to keep it away. I didn't want the pleasure-filled high to end, and because I'd staved it off, a greedy orgasm tore through me. It ripped into me so badly that it made me scream out, and I didn't care where we were. I called for him, and he answered by jackhammering into me like he couldn't get enough.

Harder and harder. Faster and faster until another orgasm tore through me, severing me from this reality. Taking me to a place I never wanted to leave. It was just the two of us, and I didn't want it to be any other way.

I felt his climax grip me. He pumped harder still,

then tightened his grip on my hips until it was almost painful. Then he slowed to an even pace and stopped.

Pat pulled me closer, holding me against his chest. We were both breathing hard.

In the bright sunlight, I could just make out the shadow of our reflection.

His sun-kissed skin against my dark skin. It was a beautiful combo.

"Come home with me," he whispered against my hair.

"Home?" I managed.

"That was unreal, amazing. I need more. More of you. Much more of you." He bent down and kissed the groove between my neck and shoulder.

"Can I confess that I need you too?" My heart expanded and melted.

"You can. I want you to."

"I'm confessing."

He laughed, and his hot, warm breath tickled my skin.

"So, what percentage of you was that?

"Thirty-five," I teased. I was making myself sound like some sort of temptress diva.

"Fuck… I want to get you to at least seventy-five by Friday night."

"Friday night?"

"We'll be out of the office for the rest of the week. You better not hold back."

I laughed. "I don't plan to."

CHAPTER 19

Patterson

THE BEAUTIFUL GODDESS sat in my kitchen.

I'd stolen the title of Goddess for my girl. Sure, I agreed wholeheartedly that Jada was a goddess, but this woman here was mine.

I had my very own woman of angelic beauty who rocked my world and shook the ground I walked on.

This was us on Thursday morning.

We hadn't been in the office since Tuesday, and like I said, we'd be out for the rest of the week.

When last I'd checked, there were a host of messages

waiting for me and a congregation of people waiting to see me.

Dad had stopped by the apartment to check I was still alive when no one could reach either of us, and I'd spared him two minutes of time away from her.

In that two minutes, he knew two things.

The first was I was alive, and the second was I was with Georgie.

That was not planned, and right now, I didn't give a flying fuck about plans. I shoved it right to the back of my mind. Right on back there in the back of beyond.

These last few days, nothing had been more important to me than her.

Nothing at all, and I made sure she knew that.

I woke up next to her and fell asleep next to her. She was all over my dreams asleep and awake and right here in front of me now looking at me and pouting as I'd burnt the food again.

That was my third attempt. I was trying to make a Spanish omelet. I was trying to do that while feeding her strawberries, and kissing her. All at the same time. I wanted to do all of it. I loved the way she looked when she opened her mouth and took the strawberry in. And when she sucked on my fingers. Then I'd have to kiss her.

The food was a lost cause.

Every time I got the omelet going just to let it brown over, it burned crispy, beyond edible.

"Pat, either focus on the food or let me cook." She chuckled.

"No, no cooking for you. Let me try to focus."

She laughed at my show of trying to focus on her and the food.

"I'm actually so full from the fruit now."

She shuffled on the chair, showing a healthy amount of thigh.

Wearing only my shirt, she looked amazing. Her hair was in a high, messy bun piled on top of her head with loose tendrils falling down the sides, making her look sexier. Sexy, sassy, everything.

"I need to make sure you eat enough food," I insisted.

She laughed, and her eyes twinkled. "A whole tub of strawberries tends to fulfill that. Pat, you are so crazy."

Apparently, I really was crazy. Crazy for her. Obsessed with her. Maybe this was the first step before madness. I would have happily gone mad for this woman. No one would be able to tell me I hadn't fully lived because she sealed the deal of this life for me.

"Let me take care of you," she offered. "You haven't eaten yet."

Why did she have to say that? It was like everything that came out of her mouth made me want to devour her. It was like she was begging me to take her, no matter what she said.

Even if it was 'Pass the ketchup.' That sounded like 'Pass yourself' to me. 'Pass the water' was the same. 'Good night' sounded more like 'Take me.'

'Eat' sounded like she wanted me to take her again.

"Yes," I replied. "Yes please, I would love to eat you again."

She widened her eyes at me and giggled when I moved the strawberries aside and picked her up to set her on the breakfast table.

"Pat, we can't keep doing this."

"It's only Thursday, baby. We have to make the most of the week."

"The *week*? As in the whole week? Like until Sunday?"

"Baby, I don't know what's gotten into you if your week's different to mine."

She laughed some more.

As she did, I got the best idea when I saw the glorious movement of her breasts under that shirt. I had to reach out and touch them.

"Pat, are we going to be like this the whole time?"

"You have any other ideas on what we could be like?"

She thought for a moment, then shook her head. "Not really."

"Also, you're not supposed to sound like you're complaining. Are you complaining?" I frowned.

"No, I just don't want you to get in trouble at work."

Work? Of all the indecorous things she could be thinking of.

"Fuck work, baby. I don't give no part of a rat, from the head to its, ass about work. Whoever needs me can do whatever the fuck they want."

"Including Hudson and his black eye. Pat, how did he get that black eye?" She gave me a pointed stare.

I proceeded to undo the buttons on the shirt. "It was a warning to stop looking at my girl."

Her lips parted. "Pat, you didn't."

I lowered my mouth to the crook of her neck and kissed her there while I ran my fingers over her nipples to harden them.

"No more talk about Hudson, baby. I need you again."

I didn't want that name mentioned in this house or from her lips for the rest of the week.

One week. Or whatever we had from Tuesday until Sunday. Five days.

I wanted the time to be ours.

Five days for five years. The five years we'd known each other. I was going to enjoy her every day like I should have for the last five years.

She moaned as I kissed my way down to her

breasts and started sucking on the delicious globes, taking as much of the ample flesh into my mouth as I could.

Alternating from one to the other. Licking and sucking, then sucking harder, enjoying the erotic hums that fell from her lips.

I could have stayed there forever. On that thought, that idea came right back in my mind.

I moved away, releasing the diamond-hard nipples, and moved to the cupboard to grab the caramel syrup. Then to the fridge to grab a can of whipped cream.

With both in my hands, I turned back to her and she gasped.

"Patterson Flynn, what are you going to do to me?"

"Everything." I nodded and smiled.

I went back over to her and took off the shirt completely, unveiling her nakedness.

Perfect angel beauty sitting on my table like a meal waiting to be served to me.

"Oh my God," she giggled when I started spraying the cream all over her breasts. I was pretty certain I could give any dessert chef a run for their money with my skills. I covered her with the whole can, spraying her breasts and the flat plane of her stomach in swirls that swiveled and sloped.

The little temptress leaned back on the table, enjoying it too.

Next came the caramel, which I made a show of drizzling all over the cream.

I looked at the strawberry bowl and saw there were two strawberries left.

Perfect. One for each nipple.

I set them on, and she started laughing so hard that some of the cream moved.

"Hey, don't you mess up my artwork," I joked. "Breakfast time."

I didn't usually like sugar or anything sweet.

Anyone who looked at me could tell straight away that I took care of myself, ate well, and worked out.

There was nothing, however, on this earth that would stop me from licking an entire can of cream, a bottle of syrup, and two strawberries off this perfect woman laid out on my table, waiting for me to devour her.

Fuck...

This was the stuff dreams were made of. It really was.

And this was a fantasy I never, ever wanted to forget.

How Georgia French allowed me to cover her with cream and syrup and lick it off her.

God, I'll be ready to die a very happy man in about five minutes, so you can tell St. Peter to wait at the gate for me if you're ready to take me.

Time to eat.

I started with the strawberries as she watched me.

"There's no way you're going to be able to eat all that." Georgie shook her head.

"Watch me, baby, watch me."

And watch she did as I started licking and lapping up the cream from her right breast. She continued to watch until I was done and that whole area was clean, nipples pointed and thanking me for the wild suckle.

I moved to her left and did the same, loving the pleasure-filled sounds that escaped her.

She grabbed my shoulder and gasped, sucking in a sharp breath.

"Pat, I'm coming," she whimpered.

"Wait, baby. Hold it. Come when I say."

"I... can't."

"Trust me, you'll enjoy this," I promised.

I loved it even more that she listened to me.

It didn't take much effort for me to lick the rest of the cream and syrup from her. I couldn't believe I actually did it and didn't feel sick from all the cream.

With a wicked smile, I crouched down and parted her legs, ready to pleasure her a hundred percent more.

She gasped when I thrust my tongue into her pretty pussy and tightened her grip on my shoulder as I started licking and sucking at her clit.

I could have indulged in her breasts forever, but this

right here was something I could do beyond that. Eternity.

This made her mine. This made her my girl. Tasting her, tasting her and watching her fall apart before me. Watching her in the vulnerable claws of pure arousal. Watching her trust me with her body.

Trust...

She trusted me.

"Pat, I can't..."

"Come for me, Georgia," I told her, stopping my feasting to look at her. I loved saying her name. It was something that happened naturally. I tended to say it at different points over the last three weeks. When she'd first surprised me. When she'd first made my interest pique. When she'd first turned me on so bad I thought I'd explode and embarrass myself.

When I said it, it felt like I was speaking to some internal part of her that was just for me.

Her eyes held mine as she came. I returned to my tasting, allowing that sweet nectar to flow right into my mouth. I drank all of her, quenching my thirst for her.

The taste turned me on in a way I couldn't describe. I had to move quickly to the cupboard by the door separating the kitchen and the living room. It was where I kept my spare condoms.

I grabbed one and shoved it on my cock a little too

hard, and like fuck I almost embarrassed myself there again.

Taking hold of her, I guided myself into her sweet pussy and buried myself to the hilt. With all the practice we'd had over the last few days, her body welcomed me, and I was able to slide right in and start pumping into her.

I held on to her waist and went from pumps to pounding, turning myself on more by watching her perfect tits bouncing with each pound into her body.

I already knew with how much I'd enjoyed my tasting session of her that I wasn't going to last as long as I wished I could. I would, however, take whatever I could get.

"Pat..."

"I know, baby... I'm right there with you." I barely managed to speak.

It felt too good. Far too good. She felt too good, and it made me want more. I wanted more and the every-thing I'd told her I was going to do to her.

I tried to fight my release as the climax built within me like a volcano waiting to erupt. I couldn't though. Her orgasm grabbed me as it captured her and took us over the edge of reality. It sent me right over. Way over. I lost control and started jackhammering into her as I came in a hot rush. Hot and virile, erupting into her.

It took me a moment to catch my breath and steady my racing heart which was drumming in my ears.

I pulled out of her and pulled her to me the way I'd found myself doing over the last few days.

I pulled her to rest on my chest while I rested my chin on the top of her head.

My skin came alive with the passion we'd just shared. Something else happened too though. It was the moment of realization.

What was this?

What was this between us?

I wanted it, wanted it bad, but how could I have it? Inside my apartment, this was us. This was what we'd become.

Outside, and to everyone else, she was the woman who was supposedly my new toy. My new toy whom I was supposed to be getting engaged to so I could inherit the damn Flynn empire.

I took the chance to look down at her. Huge brown eyes searched mine, and it looked like she was thinking the same.

I would never know because the smoke alarm went off.

In our own smoking hot, wild lock of seriously hot sex, we didn't even notice the smoke that was starting to curl around the pan I was making the omelet in. I'd forgotten to turn the stove off.

It was billowing up now, up to the ceiling.

"Jesus." I cringed.

Georgie, however, started laughing.

"Pat, you are so crazy."

I chuckled and tilted her chin up so she could look directly at me.

"I am crazy, Georgie. For you." I kissed her, buying two more minutes before I tended to my charred omelet.

CHAPTER 20

Patterson

SUNDAY CAME, and we managed to leave the house.

I'd burnt all the food, and we'd had to order in for the last few nights.

We thought a nice lunch at our favorite restaurant would be nice.

We loved going to Big Burgers, a simple but truly fantastic diner in the city.

Nothing fancy about the place. It just had that homely comfort we liked.

It was a nice hot day, so we sat outside and ate. This would have been what we would have done last weekend. Last weekend, however, had brought its own realizations for us.

This weekend was another.

We'd finished the meal and were talking.

She was telling me about something Lana did, but I was watching her. Watching her face, watching her eyes light up every time she verged on to a topic that interested her.

"Pat, you're giving me that look again." She pouted.

"What look?"

"You're looking at me like you're studying my face." She grinned.

"What if I am? Maybe I want to commit you to memory so if I go blind, I'll remember your face."

She laughed. "That is ridiculous. You're acting like we just met."

It was like we had. "Doesn't it feel like we just did?"

The laugher receded, and she looked me over. "Yeah. It kind off does."

"I feel like I know you but I don't and I want to know more. We didn't get around to talking much about New York the other night. When you mention it I seems like you had a whole other life there that you loved." I knew it must have been important to her because of the way her eyes lit up. I knew too that she gave up her job and came back to L.A to take care of her father. "You have a marketing degree, you worked for a consultancy firm, and not any old firm either. It was a path. Then you became my PA."

"I did. New York was a different life for me."

I'd never stopped to think that she might want to go back into marketing. I had been too selfish to consider it. I'd just assumed that since I paid her good money, I was the better option to stick with.

That brought me back to the recent situation. With two million dollars, what would keep her with me?

As if on cue with my thoughts, I heard a camera clicking. She turned at the same time as me to see a man with no shame whatsoever walk right up to us and start taking pictures. He came from across the street near the jewelers.

We both watched him until he was done. I'd learned never to engage or say anything.

Georgie looked back at me as the man walked away.

"I guess that was a reminder of our plan," she sighed. "We need to go back to the office with something big."

It didn't feel right anymore. It hadn't felt right in the first place, but at least back then it had felt like a plan my best friend was helping me out with. I hadn't even thought of her as my PA back then.

"What?" she asked.

I didn't know if I could continue with the plan, but saying that to her would take away from what she would have planned to do with the money. I couldn't do that.

I would sooner just give her the money because it wasn't like I didn't have it to give. But I knew her. She wouldn't take it. She was the type of woman who worked for her money, and with such a large amount, she wouldn't have wanted to feel obligated to me in any way.

I had to say something though, something meaningful, because she was looking at me.

"Feels weird, Georgie. My family will all think I'm with you because of some crazy demand my father placed on me, but even if I tell them, it will always feel like they didn't believe me. They won't know I'm with you because I want to be."

Maybe it was too soon to say that, because something I couldn't quite work out flickered in her eyes.

"You're thinking about that?" She looked surprised.

"Of course, I am. You know what kind of scandal the papers would come up with if they knew?"

"They'll never know. You know they'll never hear it from me. Or Lana. She would take my secrets to the grave." She nodded.

The person I was worried about was her. Georgie. Her.

"You'll know. You'll know the truth, and there will be nothing anyone can tell you to refute that. You said it yourself. I'm selfish and manipulative. You had to make me promise there would be no whores so you'd be with me."

She shook her head at me. "Pat, stay focused. We can deal with the details later. I agree. Your dad was way out of line by making a demand like that on you. I think he did it to teach you some kind of lesson. That was my take on it. He used the situation and your desperation to his advantage to get you to do something he wants badly for you. You work hard, and I wouldn't be any kind of friend if I allowed you to lose everything."

All I heard was 'friend', and that was enough to give me palpitations.

"*Friend?* Georgie, for the love of God, don't tell me you just want to be my friend."

She laughed again and reached across the table to take my hand. "I'm sorry, I think I officially broke up with you as my friend on Thursday, and that was after sleeping with you twenty-two and half times."

"Half?"

"I fell asleep. I don't think it counts."

I smirked. "It counts, baby. One of us was still working hard."

"Okay, so twenty-three times, then," she amended. "Plus, after you covered me in cream and syrup and licked me clean, that pretty much threw friendship to the wind. The thought that I want you to do that to me again was the cherry on top. So, when I say 'friend,' I mean back then *then*."

"We need more cream, and I'll cover you with chocolate and hazelnut syrup this time, and that bronze stuff you put on your skin to make the whole thing sparkle."

Later. I would do that to her as soon as we stepped in the house.

"Oh my God, Pat. You're terrible. Anyway, rolling back to what I was saying before we started talking about our plans for later, I want you to have what you deserve. That I get two million I would have never made in my lifetime is an added bonus." She did that one-shoulder sassy shrug thing.

That thought returned to my mind. The thought about her and money. Then there was what Ivan had said too.

I could ask her now what she would use it for. It was on the tip of my tongue to ask, but the sense of inappropriacy came back to me.

If she wanted to, she would have said what she was going to do with it. Just then, she could have followed up that remark with what she planned to do. Asking would be ... well, it didn't feel right.

I noticed the way she said it though. She showed more emotion talking about why she wanted to help me. She showed more emotion on that than talking about the money.

"I have an idea." She beamed, glancing over at the jewelry store.

The jewelry store that sold engagement rings.

I followed her gaze, then looked back to her. "Jewelry store equals engagement ring."

She nodded. "We're three weeks away from the fundraiser. It would be perfect and oh so believable. We both disappear from the office for a week. Then we come back engaged." She squealed.

That was entirely believable and such a good plan I had to give her complete credit.

"I love it. I'm not getting your ring from there though." Nice as the store was, it seemed a little on the cheaper side. The kind of place we'd go to if we were both eighteen and had no real money.

"What's wrong with it? They look cool enough for something that would work for what we want," she argued.

I had to laugh. "This may be a plan we rigged up, but I'm getting you the ring I'd get you if I asked you outside this plan."

A curious look formed in her eyes. "Lord have mercy, Pat, what are you saying to me? What kind of ring would you get me?"

"Come on, looks like we have to head to Beverly Hills."

Her mouth dropped.

"*What?* No, Pat, I'm fine with something quaint and dainty."

No time to argue. We had a lot to do today.

Head to the stores for more cream and syrup, and her ring.

I'd get the best.

I stood up and moved over to her. She laughed when I scooped her up out of her chair and heaved her over my shoulder caveman style.

"Come on, Mrs. Flynn. Let's go get your ring."

Mrs. Flynn.

It felt so right to say that.

We got to Tiffany's on Rodeo Drive and I couldn't remember ever seeing Georgia look so excited.

If I'd known she was going to be like this I would have brought her here every week.

A cascade of diamonds greeted us when the store assistant took us over to the glass cases containing the engagement rings.

I wanted to be excited too but I couldn't get rid of

that voice in the back of my mind telling me this was fake and all of this was for show.

Only God knew how many people had gotten pictures of us going in the store, so it was God's guess as to what would be in the papers tomorrow.

"I don't know what to do with myself." Georgie gasped looking around at everything. Her eyes sparkled just as much as the diamonds.

"Did you have anything particular in mind?" The assistant asked. She was a middle aged woman with a neat up do and a smile that reminded me of Mom's.

It was the smile that was reserved for the couples in love, who came here because they wanted the best.

Well since I wanted Georgie to have the best I decided to keep that in mind when she looked at me.

"We'll take your best ring please," I told her.

The woman laughed. "Mr. Flynn while that sounds perfect. It's not that simple. they're all good. it just depends on what you think she would like. The fact that she's here is great. Have you already proposed?"

I looked back to Georgie who looked even more nervous.

"No. Not yet. I'm waiting for the right moment." I answered. When was the right moment to do this sort of thing?

All I knew was it was supposed to be special and memorable.

"Oh wonderful, okay, let me show you what we have that I would consider the best."

I took Georgie's hand as the woman walked around a corner to a display of rings that sparkled so brightly it hurt my eyes.

Georgie leaned closer to me and tugged on my arm, pulling me down to whisper into my ear.

"These are too much Pat." She shook her head.

I just smiled at her. "Nothing's too much for you."

She winced and we both looked over to where the lady stood.

We followed at stopped at a display where all the rings looked like they could have been made for her.

There was one though one I saw and she saw at the same time.

It was so striking that she left my side and walked over to it as if she were in some sort of daze.

"Wow well it looks like we have a winner." The woman smiled.

"Could I see that one please."

"Of course," the woman went around the counter and took the ring out of the display unit.

I walked up to Georgie and she looked over to me.

"That looks like you." I smiled at her.

"You think so?"

"Yup, that is totally you." The ring was a princess cut

setting with diamonds going around the pavilion. It was beautiful, just like her.

Fuck. Listen to me and look where I was.

The woman handed me the ring to put it on Georgie. I slipped it on her finger. It was slightly too big, but damn was it ever her.

"Oh my God, it's so beautiful." She smiled.

"You want that one?"

She looked away bashful but I cupped her face and guided her back to me.

"Georgia French if you want that ring, tell me."

"Yes. I really like this one." She bubbled trying to tamp down her excitement.

"It's all yours." I lowered to kiss her and realized something. This felt real.

It felt real because it was real.

We did this part my way and I'd do the proposal my way too.

Not in public for all to see.

Somewhere where it was just the two of us.

The best place I could think of was back at my place.

When we got home I led her out to the terrace, near the water fountain she loved.

"Now?" she laughed.

"Yeah, now."

"No one can see us." she pointed out.

I took the ring from my back pocket and lowered to

one knee. If anyone told me I would be doing this right now I would never have believed them.

"No one needs to. This is just for us."

She looked at me, really looked at me and the emotion in her eyes was all there.

I popped open the box and she smiled at the ring.

"Georgia Maria French," I began. At first I was thinking of saying all the wonderful things there was to say about her. Then my heart took over. "I remember the first day I met you. I didn't know you were going to have such an impact on my life. I didn't know how priceless you would become to me. I can't live without you. Please be mine."

Please be mine...

There that was the part that was real. I didn't ask her to marry me. I didn't ask her to be my wife I asked her to be mine. An engagement ring would say it all but asking her to be mine spoke of the real part of what I was doing.

"Yes." She bubbled and nodded.

As I slipped the ring on her finger, she felt like mine.

CHAPTER 21

Georgia

Looks like this one's for Keeps...

Sorry girls, looks like Patterson Flynn is off the market completely and no longer one of LA's finest Bachelor's. He got engaged to Georgia French two weeks ago and the two are in a world of their own...

Melanie Curtis, The Chronicle

That was the headline and first paragraph of the front page of The Chronicle.

Under that was a the picture of Pat and me from two weeks ago inside Tiffany's and a picture of us from yesterday walking in the park holding hands.

We were completely oblivious to everything and everyone. I didn't bother to read the papers anymore. This was from Lana. She showed it to me.

We sat in her living room feet up on the sofa with a rerun of America's next Top Model playing in the background.

I got here about half an hour ago. As usual all the talk was about Pat.

"It's sweet isn't it?" Lana commented glancing over at the paper.

I was still holding it, looking at Pat and me.

I set if down on the coffee table.

"It is sweet." The papers weren't as mean as that first one that called me a toy.

"Forget being with a rock star. I can't believe you guys got so much publicity. I love it though. It's made you face something you stayed away from for years." Lana smiled. Her hoop earrings dangled and she nodded.

"I know. I'm so different to what I was even a few months ago. My life feels like it just took a turn into an unexpected path I would never have gone down."

She straightened up and reached out her hand to me. "Let me see it again."

My ring. She was talking about my ring. My ring that had caught everyone's attention. Everyone wanted to see it .

They all wanted to see the ring Pat paid seven hundred and fifty thousand dollars for.

I couldn't believe I was wearing a rock that cost close to a million dollars on my hand when I needed money for other things.

I knew it wasn't about that, and he wanted to get the best for me. it was just a weird feeling. One that I allowed myself to treasure.

I put out my hand to her and she smiled the same way she did when she first saw it.

"It's so beautiful Georgie." She brought her hand to her heart and smiled wider. "Girl, how are you feeling about it all? The fundraiser is on Saturday."

"The fundraiser is on Saturday." I repeated bringing my hands up to my cheeks. It was unbelievable how the time had come around so fast.

"It's like you blinked and skipped over weeks. I wish I could be there just to see what happens." Lana was going to be in Milan prepping for fashion week. I was used to her travelling at various times during the year but this was possibly the one time I wished she was going to be around.

"Lana, I don't even know what's happening." I chuckled on edge. "We're just going to see what happens on the day and take it from there. The best part is we're engaged. The original plan was to do that this week, but we've been engaged for two weeks now."

"You guys are like … a real couple."

I pulled in a deep breath. "Yeah."

We felt real and everyone was happy for us like we were real. When I told Dad we were engaged he cried.

Two weeks might have passed but it felt like minutes ago that Pat proposed to me. It was what he said. I absolutely noticed that he took care I what he said to me. he asked me to be his.

He wasn't pretending to do anything. It wasn't a pretend proposal it was him being real with me. On the outside though it was fake. Nothing could really change that and I'd gotten to the stage where it was starting to bother me.

It bothered me but I guess not enough to stop me from running with my plans.

Dad was scheduled for surgery in a month. Dr. Thompson put him on a strict diet I prep for that and all was going well on that front. I'd also viewed a bungalow style house on the beach for him.

With everything on the ground floor he wouldn't have to worry about any stairs.

I put my name down to discuss making an offer on the place. There was one other place I had to view but I knew the beach house suited dad more.

Then for me, there was the property on Santa Monica Blvd.

There was an open house on Wednesday for it. After waiting so long I couldn't believe this was happening.

A vision of something I wanted and thought I wouldn't be able to get all coming true. Well, hopefully. It was an open house so I'd have to put an offer there on the place that night.

It was really jumping the gun and counting my chickens before they hatched but, I had to act. I knew that place would get snapped up the minute it became available.

So far everything had gone smooth with Pat. I couldn't see any reason why there would be any hiccups.

"Have you told him about your plans. I know you were worried about that but is it different now?" Lana asked.

"I haven't said anything." I shook my head. "I still feel the same. It's going to be hard to tell him I'm going into this business venture and I won't be his PA anymore."

"Georgie I'm pretty certain he knows you won't need a job with all that money you'll be getting."

"Of course. It's just weird. I feel like I'm leaving him."

"You'll still be his girl Georgie." She grinned. "even I've noticed how much he's changed and the way he looks at you, you can tell he's only into you. I just can't believe he's the same person."

I couldn't believe a person could change that much in such a short space of time.

It all looked like it was part of this plan, but if I was being honest I saw him change for us.

I hoped like hell I wasn't in some bubble and it would pop and land me on my ass and then reality would rear its ugly head and call me foolish for believing pat could change.

"It's hard to get my head around. All of it. Him, and my business." I couldn't believe I was in a position to even be looking at the property.

"Georgie it's your dream. Just talk to him about it. it feels like some secret your keeping and it shouldn't be."

" I think that my marketing business was a thing I held so dear to me that I dare not speak about it with anyone besides you. You were the only one I told about setting up something small, and you were the only one I told about Marsha and all my other clients."

"I get it, but I think he'd be happy for you."

"I'll tell him. I'll find the right time. it's not like it's going to happen overnight. we have to get this wedding out of the way first."

"God. That is a lot. So many plans."

So many plans with a host of things to arrange. We

hadn't even agreed on a date yet for the wedding. I could always tell when he was thinking the same as me.

Engagement, wedding, then divorce.

Divorce...

It made my stomach twist into knots.

What would happen then? What would happen to us?

Then it would be all over the papers, just like us getting together. The papers would jump on that story fast and make it a scandal. That was what they would do. then people would think it was weird if we were still together.

Getting together for real wasn't part of the plan. That part wasn't supposed to happen. It was something that neither of us saw coming.

I definitely hadn't seen it in the works or the cards for either of us.

I wasn't supposed to feel this way about him.

I wasn't supposed to fall for him.

There was no point telling myself that I hadn't, or shouldn't. I did.

I fell for Patterson Flynn somewhere along the line and now it was too late to try to go back on all the things I cautioned myself.

Too late to say don't fall for him.

"Lana, I'm actually scared. We moved to phase two,

what now? This really is a mess and I think it's going to get messier."

What I meant was messy in terms of emotion. I didn't want to get hurt. I really didn't want to get hurt.

I'd opened my heart to Pat. Saw past all the things I hated that he'd done in the past, and got to this point where I was with him.

The uncertainty however was getting to me. I didn't like that part. It was something too that neither of us could really talk about as it was one of those things you had to experience and move to the next square based on what you learned while you were in the situation.

She shook her head. "Georgie, my dear friend. I know what you're saying and if it were me I would be scared too. But I think you should remember that you guys control what happens next. That really could mean anything, but you control it. Just for the record though, I really think you guys make a good couple and I'm routing for you."

Me too. I was routing for us too.

I just didn't know it things were going to be as simple as controlling what happens next.

I had a feeling it wouldn't be and the feeling ate away at my insides.

CHAPTER 22

Patterson

As usual mom made the very best meal ever.

Lasagna. Her perfect lasagna. Made with vine tomatoes from the garden and exotic herbs and spices. To add to that she'd made a peach flan which was some healthy version so she used some oatmeal base instead of the traditional sponge base. It was divine.

I ate like a horse.

Last week Georgie joined us for dinner and my parents loved her company.

Today was one of Dad's business dinner's where he wanted to talk to me.

Dinner first, talking next.

I wished it was the other way around because you could leave dinner as soon as you finished. However, I knew he did it this way on purpose.

Having the meeting after meant I'd have to wait until we finished dinner to find out what he wanted to discuss. Eating first meant we could meet together as a family just like when I was a kid.

It was eight now. Mom said goodnight and left us men to speak in Dad's office.

Dad took out a Cuban cigar and lit it up, holding it up between his thumb and forefinger like he was the Godfather.

I laughed when he took a draw and released the smoke.

"Your mother almost killed me when she found out I offered you one of these." He chuckled.

"I remember." I was eighteen and that was supposed to be my initiation to manhood. In actual fact the only thing he did was put me off smoking for life.

I never touched a cigarette and I never went near another cigar.

It was vile. Vile as shit, or what I imagined shit to taste like.

Aside from making me cough my insides out it made me sick.

"We've come a long way since boy. A long way since

you were that crazy eighteen year old conjuring all manner of plans to make me crazy."

If he looked a little deeper I knew he'd find I wasn't all that different to that crazy eighteen year old boy I used to be conjuring plans to make him crazy.

I just got better at it and conjured the mother of all plans.

A plan I was in the full swing of and starting to feel the guilt of.

"I'm proud of you." dad added, adding to my guilt.

"Really?"

"Patterson, I know my demand to find a wife in six weeks was off the charts ridiculous but it was my way. I needed you to calm down and you did. I needed you to be serious and be the leader I knew you could be and you really stepped up. Most of all though I don't think I could be more proud that you and Georgie are engaged. Secretly I kind of hoped you'd pursue her but I didn't want to say. You did it though."

That actually surprised me. "I did."

"Any plans on a wedding date?"

"Well it has to be soon right?" I chuckled.

"I'm sure if there were any setbacks we could work around it. I'm convinced you're in love and you pursued a woman that was marriage material. I'm happy with that." Dad nodded.

"You're convinced we're in love?" I was really interested to hear what he thought.

"You can't fake that. You can pretend all you want with other stuff but the eyes give you away. it's true what they say. They really are windows to the soul. It also takes one to know one and I'm perpetually in love with your mother. I see love when you look at Georgie and I see the same thing when she looks at you. Treasure that son. Always remember that no matter what happens, because it will be all you have as evidence to know it was real."

Normally when Dad talked like this I would zone out. I didn't have a reason to listen before now. I'd groan inwardly and cringe that he was talking about something that didn't interest me.

Nothing was further from the truth tonight.

"Thanks dad. I appreciate that a lot."

He nodded. "I know the men in our family haven't been the best examples for you. I'm very aware of what a lot of them get up to but each to their own. I hope you won't be like that. I hope you respect your wife and make sure she knows she's the most important thing to you in this world. Make sure you know money is second. It's great when you have it sure, but you can't take it with you. those things are temporary. Love is different."

"Okay dad. I hear ya." Message received loud and clear, adding to my guilt.

"I hope so boy. Anyway, that was only a part of the business talk. I wanted to talk to you about the Miami Beach project. I loved what you said in the meeting. That is exactly what I felt about the place when you first told me about it. Miami Beach is beautiful. That landfill scarred the land. As property developers we see the vision of what a place can potentially be. It's creativity and imagination. You have all of that. I see no reason to wait until Saturday to do this so I'm officially handing over the project to you as of now."

My mouth fell open and I just stared at him. "Dad, really?"

"Yeah. A few days early isn't going to make that much of a difference. It's all your and I've transferred the five million forecast capital into your account so you can get on to it straight away to do as you wish. Let's face it, the place was yours at the start anyway."

I smiled, unable to tamp down the excitement that flowed through me.

"My God dad. That's more than what I could have imagined."

"Engagement present." Dad chuckled.

I had a plan. I was going to give Georgie her money before the fundraiser. I'd give her the whole two million. It wasn't like I needed to stagger anything. I would give it to her as my own engagement present to her.

I'd feel better in some respect and I knew that would make her happy to have that.

Damn, maybe then I'd get to see what she'd do with and answer my long awaited question.

"Thank you. Thanks so much I'm grateful and I'll take this project and the company to the next level." I had some serious plans for Miami Beach. I would more than take it to the next level.

More important was that it was mine.

"I know you will." He chuckled. "Let's be grateful I'm as crazy as you and had the good sense to demand you find a marriable woman in six weeks."

I laughed but my laugher dissipated when someone behind me cleared their throat.

I turned and my whole body cringed when I saw Hudson at the door.

Fuck.

How long had he been standing there?

What did he hear? Did he hear what dad just said?

Hudson was a snake. A snake waiting to attack its prey.

The look on his face told me he'd heard something.

"Hudson, I wasn't expecting you." Dad said.

"I was on my way back from the fundraiser venue and thought I'd stop by to see if you were okay. You said you were feeling faint earlier." Hudson answered. He cut me a sharp glance.

"Oh God, it was because I didn't have lunch." Dad chuckled. "You okay?"

"You know what? I am." Again he looked at me and I wondered what the hell he would do with the information.

It could mean nothing. As far as anyone knew Georgie and I were engaged. That was the end of the story. No one knew intricate details.

I just had to keep it that way.

CHAPTER 23

Georgie

I JUST KNEW I was going to fall in love with this place.

I did months ago when I first saw images of it come on the market.

That was when the property had been cleaned out and the owners wanted to get a feel of interest.

I heard that over a hundred people made an expression of interest. That included me with all my financial restraints at the time.

I just wanted to go and see the place even if there was no hope for me to buy it or get a mortgage on it. The mortgage was what I was hoping for because I knew there would be no way on earth that I'd have the kind of money they were setting down at the starting offer price for the place.

Today I was here in the building amongst a few other interested parties viewing the place at this very elaborate open house where I was served a glass of wine on entry.

I was here, and I Georgia French was going to put the offer in at what the owners wanted, paid in cash. There would be people here that may haggle to get it down lower. Others who would most likely put in an offer at above the offer price.

If that happened I would be alerted and given the chance to outbid them.

The type of people here that I'd seen so far were all wealthy. I could tell straight away and I knew none of them would be going via the mortgage option. This was Santa Monica Blvd. People around these parts didn't worry about a budget.

They didn't need to and this place was the kind of set up where you would pay whatever the asking price was if it was in line with your vision.

It was definitely in line with mine.

The store front had that chic look most business places had with the floor to ceiling windows which I planned to leave clear so potential clients could see inside.

I also planned to have the sign with the business name done very elegant and simple.

The color scheme of the interior was a very attractive feature so I would be keeping that. There was an open plan section that could fit four to six desks. That was perfect since I planned to hire two other consultants, a receptionist and a secretary. Working for Pat taught me that you needed enough people to do different things. Even if it looked like one person's job was too easy to justify. Like having a receptionist separate to the secretary. The receptionist would answer phone calls and deal with clients wouldn't just walked in off the street, while the secretary would do the administrative tasks.

I wanted one consultant to manage the campaigns alongside me and the other to outsource new businesses. So someone who would be looking around at potential clients and also help to get the word out about us.

I was very proud to say that I'd drawn up a whole plan and it looked like it would do well. I just needed to get this place. it didn't take all that long to look around but what took up time was filling out the paperwork.

We were given the option to take it away and send it in or go online and fill it in , or hand it in now. I chose the latter because I wanted to get in. Get myself ahead of the game. Since the owners were very particular about the place and who they were going to sell to there were a number of questions on the forms that I didn't really expect to see.

They wanted to know what sort of business I wanted to set up. What plans I had so far. If I was already established, my annual turnover to date and things like that. since I already had everything committed to memory and I was so passionate about what I wanted to do I was able to write it all down.

I just handed it in and thought I'd have one last look so I went on the second floor to the room I saw as my office. It was beautiful and perfect. I gazed out the window and looked around at the other office buildings and stores.

I could imagine me all set up in here doing well for myself. Getting ahead in life and doing what I dreamed of doing back in high school.

"Great view," said a voice from behind me.

I expected to see one of the other people who'd come to look at the place. I was completely thrown, however, to see Hudson standing behind me.

Hudson Flynn, live and in living color. Standing paces away from me. Wearing that same leery smirk he had on his face when he asked me to go back to his hotel room two years ago while we were at a business conference and get up close and personal with his massive cock.

That was what the man said to me.

From that day I never spoke to him. Prior to that I was respectful because of who he was, respectful in Pat's presence and especially in Richard's.

After that proposition I decided I didn't have to speak to him to work with him, because I didn't work for him. We could co-exist in the same building.

The same building as in anything to do with Flynn's.

Not here. What was he doing here?

Okay... stupid question. This was an open house and anyone could be here.

Him though? Why did the universe hate me?

"I don't think I've congratulated you personally yet on your engagement to my cousin. I can't wait to see how this pans out." He smiled wider and gave me a devilish look.

"Is there some point to congratulating me and not meaning it?" I asked in a cool, casual manner. No point showing him he got under my skin. No point showing that part of me. It was that weakness again. Showing weakness and falling prey to something bigger than me.

He chuckled. "Am I that transparent?"

"Look, you have no reason to talk to me. I have no reason to talk to you. We aren't at work. So, if you could please just leave me alone I would be very grateful." I was trying to go for a tactful way to get rid of him, but it didn't work.

The asshole took that as an invitation to come closer to me. I stepped back into the corner and he put out his hand on the wall to block my escape.

"Why are you here Georgie? I didn't hear any talk of this place on the plans," he said just above a whisper.

"Why are you here?" I shot back.

"I followed you. simple. wanted to see what my cousin's new sexy fiancée was up to." When his gaze fell to my breasts it made me sick. "What business would she have on a place like this?"

"It's nothing to do with you."

He laughed. "Maybe not, but hey… couldn't resist the chance to rattle your bones. There's something not quite right here, and I'm going to find out what it is. Until then know this, you may be all loved up now but Patterson Flynn will never be serious about you. It's in the blood. We can't just settle with one woman. It's not enough and you aren't enough. You'll just be something good to look at. A piece of ass to fuck. When he's finished with you, he'll just toss you to the wayside and find the next piece of ass."

I sucked in a sharp breath, stunned and hurt by his words.

Stunned and hurt, and unable to say anything because the worse kind of accusations were the ones that held a big element of truth.

I knew Pat. I knew him and that was what he did.

"Leave me alone." I shook my head at him. The backs of my eyes stung.

"You know I'm right. You know him more than me so you must know I'm right. He'll never be serious about you, marriage or not. He's not serious about anyone. You are no different. When you see sense come find me, the offer's still up to get up close and personal with my dick."

I didn't care how I looked, I pushed him hard away from me. he moved and I practically fled the premises.

I ran to my car and drove. Drove with no destination in mind.

I should tell Pat that I saw Hudson. I should tell him what he said to me. I should tell him that Hudson suspected something was up with us and our whole plan could go to hell.

I didn't know if I could find the strength though, because through all of that it was the first time I'd heard someone tell me that Pat would never be serious about me.

It cut me deep because it was a fear I'd had from the beginning when I knew I first had feelings for him. It was something that cut deeper too, because I knew it was true. That was why I placed that guard up all these years. that was why I never allowed myself to see us as anything other than professional.

That was why I protected my heart which didn't just dream of really getting the chance to launch my career.

It dreamed of him too.

I must have drove around for an hour mindlessly before I ended up pulling into the parking lot of Pat's place.

I didn't plan to come here tonight but here I was. My heart led me straight to him.

He was in the gym working out.

When I saw him a tear ran down my cheek and he stopped his bicep curls to rush over to me when he saw how upset I was.

"Baby what's wrong with you?"

Where did I start?

When I thought about it this was one of those situations where a little thing could turn into something big. Me keeping my plans to myself were exactly that. I wanted to do what I was doing and share them with him when the time was right.

Hudson would figure it out. I knew he would. The people at the open house were there to buy the place. It would be clear that I had the same intention and the looming question over me being there would be where I got money like that from. What if he guessed?

I would have messed everything up for Pat.

"Pat, I have to tell you something."

"What, what happened?" He looked worried.

"Hudson…"

"What did he do?" Anger blazed in Pat's eyes, worse than I'd ever seen.

The part of the conversation that bothered me the most was the least of our worries. All that stuff about Pat not being serious about me was nothing in comparison to what Hudson would do if he figured out what we planned and used it to destroy Pat. I owed it to him to give him a heads up.

"I think I messed things up. Hudson didn't do anything to me." Technically that was a lie, but I would let his proposition run off my back like water. "I planned to use the money to get Dad a place because he's been very sick and can't continue to live where he is. I also planned to use the money to help launch my career. I was going to tell you when the time was right. Hudson followed me to the open house of a place I was interested in. It cost a fortune. He's going to wonder how I came by all that money. If he figures it out he'll know."

I couldn't believe I was able to blurt all that in one babble. There was so much emotion to it, so much I banked on it and I was able to tell him.

To my surprise he cupped my face. "Don't worry

baby. There's always a way around stuff. I'll figure it out. Leave Hudson to me."

"Pat he said there's something up with us and he'll figure it out. I don't want you to lose what you worked so hard for." More tears ran down my cheek.

"Georgie, how can you worry about me when you're dad's so sick? Why didn't you tell me? Why wouldn't you tell me that, and your career stuff?" He gazed down at me.

I couldn't answer. I didn't know what to say that wouldn't add to how bad it looked that I hadn't said anything.

"Pat, I'm sorry. I am. I have these weird beliefs that I should keep certain things to myself but on this occasion I should have told you. I just don't want my plans to ruin yours. What if he figures it out?"

"What? What will he figure out? What is there to figure out? Aren't we real Georgie?" It was a question that hit me hard.

Just for a moment the question made me forget. I forgot everything and all I could see was the intense look in his eyes that begged me to say yes.

It was real for me. It was definitely real for me.

"Yes."

He continued his gaze, staring at me like he could see straight into my heart and soul. His eyes searched mine and he bent his head down to press his forehead to mine.

"It's real for me Georgie." He whispered paralyzing me further, freezing time, freezing everything. That was the moment I felt the last shred of resolve slip away from me. My last ounce of control over my heart. The last ounce of what I held on to, to protect myself from truly and utterly falling in love with this man.

It happened right there and all that I felt for him flowed through me. I'd felt an ounce of it before today. Enough to be able to admit to myself that I'd fallen for him.

This was different.

It was love.

Pure, true. It was love.

He moved to my lips and kissed me hard. Kissing me like he never kissed me before and I kissed him back with reckless abandon.

He picked me up and carried me up to the bedroom, settling me down on the bed where he stripped my clothes off and shrugged out of his.

Hot, greedy kisses were placed all over my body. I could feel him everywhere, all over me. Inside my soul and over my whole body as it came alive with everything. His touch, his kiss, his need for me.

My body welcomed him as he slid into me and we

got lost in the mad rhythm of our passionate lovemaking.

That was all I was aware of. After that it was raw emotion.

Every touch was filled with that passion and desire. Magic and fire all blended into one and I realized we weren't just getting lost in the wild sex we'd had over the last few weeks. he was making love to me.

Pat was making love to me and I was making love to him.

Nothing else seemed to matter. As we came we surrendered to the call of the force that had taken us.

It devoured us both and sent us right over the edge of ecstasy.

Nothing could stop me from going over, and him right alongside me.

Nothing.

It was ultimate pleasure and everything amazing rolled into one.

It was so powerful that we both had to catch our breath and he crumpled next to me , our bodies dripping with sweat.

As usual he pulled me flush against his chest and held me there.

"I love you." he whispered against my hair.

He'd told me that before, just not in that way. When he said it before he meant he loved me the way a friend would. I never even considered at the time that those words were hard to say to anyone friend or not. And I'd never said it back to him, because usually when he said it to me there was some kind of craziness I'd have to deal with.

Just now when he said it, he said it the way a man would when he loved a woman, and it brought reality home to me.

"I love you too." I told him, because it was true. It always was.

I rested my head against his chest listening to the strong beat of his heart.

Love...

It was such a delicate thing. Sometimes it could over power many things. sometimes it could not.

In the last few minutes I felt both aspects of it.

I felt that Pat loved me, but Hudson's words came rushing back into my mind.

He'd never be serious about you. He's not serious about anyone. You are no different...

That was what he said in a nutshell.

Truths. All truths. Pat, love, and Pat's personality.

I knew it to be true, because no one knew this man more than me.

CHAPTER 24

Patterson

THE AIR around me was pregnant with anticipation.

The tension was just around me though. Everyone else seemed fine and went about their day like nothing in particular was happening.

Maybe that was what their world was like.

Me on the other hand…

Well, there was a chance that I could have come to that point where things were about to blow up in my face.

When Georgie told me what happened I experienced a range of emotions.

It wasn't a good feeling. I was thrown that she didn't tell me about her father and her plans for her career, livid that Hudson followed her despite my warning to him weeks ago, and lastly I felt guilty that I dragged her into a messy situation.

I guess I knew what she needed the money for now, and it wouldn't be her alone that would make Hudson figure anything out. He'd heard what Dad said last night. He'd heard him say that we could be grateful he was as crazy as I was to insist on me finding a wife.

That would have stirred suspicion. I didn't have time to look into where Georgie had gone for the property she was interested in but I figured it must have been somewhere classy. Everything she said to be cautious of was correct because I would have jumped to those conclusions myself.

This had now turned into a game of possibility. I had to throw him off my scent somehow, someway because through all this the person I knew I'd hurt a lot was Dad.

I tricked him, and scammed him. He handed me a fortune and his demand led me to Georgie.

If anyone should tell him what was going on, it was me, and right now I was bordering on doing just that. I was bordering on coming clean.

There was something I had to do first though to test the waters.

I came in with Georgie and headed up here while she went to her office.

I headed up to the executive floor and went straight to Hudson's office. When he came here this was where he do his work from.

He was the only one of the cousins who had a designated office because he came here regularly. The others shared an office on a need to use basis.

His was open and the prick was inside going through paperwork.

When he saw me, he had the audacity to smile.

Smile like he knew he had me right where he wanted me.

I walked in and closed the door. The notion made him smile even more.

"I was wondering when you'd make an appearance," he taunted.

"Oh yeah?" I asked in a cool voice like I wasn't ready to beat him to a pulp. "Thought I told you to stay away from my girl."

"You did, I just didn't listen. You know what Patterson, I really have to give you credit. It turns out you can sink lower than me so congratulations."

"I'm nothing like you."

"No, I don't think I would have thought up the concoction you did. I figured it out. I figured it all out. I knew something was off the whole time because Uncle

Richard never told me what he asked you to do, and the fact that I was even here was a sign that something was wrong."

"There's nothing wrong."

"Keep telling yourself that. I walked in at the perfect moment to hear him tell you he'd insisted on you getting a wife. Then it dawned on me. Your PA, you two got together really fast like you had some time scale you were working on. It was weird you even being with a woman like that because she knows you so well. I didn't believe in the change of heart and the flirty sessions. And bam, this engagement only weeks later after I get here." He gave me a dubious look. "Come on Patterson. I'm not stupid. I'm guessing you were supposed to find a wife the natural way and you paid your PA to scheme with you so you could get the empire."

"Fucking asshole." My skin prickled and my nerves scattered at the thought of him guessing the truth.

"Me, the asshole? Really look at this." He held up a piece of paper and slammed it down on the desk.

I picked it up. it was a proposal for an offer on a commercial property on Santa Monica Blvd. This was the place Georgie wanted and according to this she was willing to pay the asking price of four hundred and fifty thousand. I didn't know how he got his hands on this. It looked like a print out.

"I know you pay her well, but damn you must either

pay her a fortune a year for her to have that kind of money up front. Or, you paid her to do something for you. like be your fake fiancée?"

This was make or break. I could crumble and allow him to win, that would drag Georgie deeper into this shit. Or, I could put him in his place.

I walked up to him and slammed the paper down. Another lie would be told today.

"I gave her the money, you asshole. I gave her the money. And I don't know what sort of ass backwards plan you think I brewed but you're wrong."

"You would have hit me by now if I was wrong." He threw back and I answered that with a punch in his face that stunned him and sent him falling back off his chair.

I moved around to his sorry ass and grabbed him the same way I did the other day.

"Is that better?" I taunted.

"Patterson, you fucker. I'm no fool. You can say whatever you want but I know you."

"I've known her for five years. Dad told me to find a wife and I have. She's the woman I'm engaged to. I just opened my eyes to what was in front of me." That was true. There was no part of that, that was a lie. I just left off certain things.

"You just expect me to believe all that? You want me to believe it's real?" he challenged.

"It is real." I balked.

"Wow, well she didn't seem to think so yesterday when I told her you would never be serious about her. She never corrected me or challenged me when I told her you've never been serious about anyone and she'd be no different. She never said anything to put me in my place because it's true Pat. That's what you're like. If it was so real she would have stood up for you and told me to go fuck myself. But don't worry I offered to take real good care of her when you get bored."

I punched him in his stomach and released him.

He laughed and I backed away.

Georgie didn't tell me any of that happened.

She never mentioned that part. She never mentioned it and I knew why.

She didn't tell me because she believed it, and I never gave her any reason to believe anything other than that.

I walked away, finished with him. I needed to see her.

I needed to find out if she really believed that. I needed to find out if she really believed she wasn't different to any other woman I'd been with.

I wanted her truth.

Her thoughts about me.

I got to her office and she stood up from her chair when she saw me.

She looked as worried as she did when we first got here.

"What happened? What did he say?" she asked, panic rose in her voice.

I looked at her and didn't know what to say first so I said the most important thing.

"Georgie, when I tell you I love you, do you believe me?"

At first she squinted like she was trying to figure out why I was asking her that. Then her lips parted and she nodded.

"I do believe you."

Okay, good. She wouldn't lie to me so I had no reason to think she was lying or telling me something she thought I wanted to hear.

"Do you think I want this relationship we have? Do you believe I'm serious about us? About you?" There that was it. it felt a lot harder in my mind to ask the question, but really it was just a few simple words.

A few simple words that required a simple yes or no answer, that she seemed pretty stuck on.

"Pat, I think you mean well. I think you want to try to believe that…"

She sounded like she was going to say *but* something or another.

"Baby, please be real with me. Be straight up with

me. I want to know how you feel. You didn't tell me everything Hudson said."

"It wasn't important." She said a little too quickly, as if she were trying to convince herself.

I shook my head. "Georgie. The whole engagement stuff he was suspicious of and any business related was the part that wasn't important. Nothing was more important than him accusing me of not being serious about you."

I spoke the words from my heart and she looked at me, but I could tell she didn't fully believe what I was saying.

She pulled in a deep breath. "Five years. I've known you for just over five years Pat, and you've always been the same. I've been right here Pat. I didn't go anywhere. I've watched you go from one woman to the next not caring who you hurt, or what you do. You think it's okay to do that because they're supposed to know from the start that you aren't serious, but it's not okay. It's not okay and I can't stand here and tell you I believe you changed for me. I can't do it. When he said what he said to me yesterday, I didn't have a leg to stand on because it was true. You just stuck around longer this time because you had something to gain. You picked me because you knew I'd do anything for you. I said yes because I was desperate. You're with me because you needed me for something. It wouldn't have happened otherwise. No matter how beautiful the relationship is that we have. It's fake."

My heart… stilled then I swore it stopped right there in my chest.

What did I expect her to say though?

What was a few short weeks in comparison to years of watching behave the same way. She didn't even have anyone to compare to, someone she'd seen me try with.

There wouldn't be anyone because I wanted her.

"Georgie… I can't begin to apologize enough and I guess I can't really get myself out of this because you know me too well. I've given you no reason to think otherwise, just my word. You're right, everything you said is completely right and I'm so ashamed of myself. I couldn't see what was in front of me this whole time. It may be completely pointless saying this but I do love you, and I think the one think you know is that I would never disappoint you. I would never hurt you. I would never…" it was pointless. It sounded like she'd already made up her mind on what she thought of me. It sounded like she'd already made up her mind about us. "We can't have a relationship where you don't trust me. Can we?"

She pressed her lips together and looked she was fighting to keep her tears away. Tears that started streaming down her cheeks.

"No," she breathed and my heart broke.

I looked at the angel in front of me and suddenly she felt so far away. So far away from me I couldn't see her.

My girl.

She didn't trust me. maybe she was right not to.

I wouldn't know what I'd do if I ever disappointed her.

Maybe it was better to leave her alone.

I turned and walked away.

CHAPTER 25

Georgie

WORDS COULDN'T QUITE DESCRIBE how bad I felt.

As I watched Pat leave it was like the world shifted around me and suddenly everything we built over the last few weeks just crumbled and feel apart.

I said no…

I told him no and it cracked us.

It felt like I threw a bolder at the bubble we'd floated in and cracked us.

I didn't know what was better continue as we were in the lie or speak up and be real with him just like he asked.

Either way, I still lost him because he was right we couldn't have a relationship where I couldn't trust him.

How could we have that? It wouldn't work.

But wasn't that just like giving up just as we'd began.

The conflict sent me straight to Dad. I went to him and before I could even say hello the tears came.

Dad was the last person I should be worrying now with my problems. He'd been doing well health wise but I had to be mindful that that didn't mean he was by any means okay.

I cried and I told him Pat and I had an argument. I never went into specific details through of the whole story. He didn't need to know that.

Telling him everything would make him feel bad that I accepted the offer of money to get married because I wanted the money. And, what did I need the money for?

Mainly for Dad.

That would lead me to telling him that my plans fell through and I might have to either get another job, move him to a care home or… well I didn't know what my other options were.

None of those sounded good.

Today taught me a lot. It told me that I didn't know if I could carry on this train of working nonstop. It was just go, go, go. Always on the move in one way or another. I couldn't keep doing it.

BELLA FONTAINE & KHARDINE GRAY

What choices did I have to lean on?

"Sweet girl, take a moment and think about this. Think you two just had an argument. That was what it was. An argument and you can talk things through." Dad nodded straightening up.

"I don't think it was just an argument Dad," I said breathlessly. "Arguing is having a disagreement about who ate the last dinner roll, who drank the last of the milk, who finished the toothpaste. Our issues were deeper."

"They're only as deep as you make them. Georgie, you knew what his past was like when you first got together. Being together was a chance for you to explore how you two felt. Do you love him?"

I nodded. "I do, but I wouldn't know what to do if he hurt me. I wish I could just not think like that."

"Georgia, maybe it's my fault why you're like this. You watched me with your mother and I knew she cheated on me and I still gave her chance after chance. It's not a good way to live. It isn't baby girl. She never once told me she would try. She just kept on with it. it's my bad for putting up with it but that doesn't have to be you. I believe that Pat wouldn't hurt you. You have to believe it too. Believing something isn't having evidence of its existence. It's knowing it's there without having to see it. that's what makes it beautiful. That's what makes a relationship worthy of love. Don't allow love to pass you by because you're scared. Believe me, you'll hate yourself for it. You'll blame yourself if you go through the next five without him wondering what could have been. I don't want that for you."

I thought about it and I didn't want that for me either. I didn't want to be that person who was left wondering what could have been. Especially when everything between Pat and me were so magical when we were together.

Could it really be as simple as just trying though?

Forget the bad stuff. Forget that I thought he wouldn't be serious about me?

If I wanted to be with him I had to.

That was what it required me to do and this was separate to the whole engagement scenario.

It existed outside it.

Dad kept his gaze trained on me. "Trust starts from inside you. you remember all the actions a person did to show you they love you, and it's just for you to believe they mean it when they say it. Believe in you guys."

"Thank you." I nodded. I appreciated him taking time to help me. "Thank you dad."

"It's just that…" he stopped talking and swayed, then brought his hand to his head.

"Dad, are you okay?"

"Um… Georgie call …911. I—" Dad tensed and the terror of my worst nightmare filled me when he grabbed his chest and fell to the ground.

"Oh God! No." no this couldn't be happening. I grabbed my phone and knelt down beside him. his eyes were closed and he looked like his breathing was slowing down.

It went from a few shallow pants to nothing.

I dialed 911 and the operator came on immediately.

"911, what's your emergency?"

As freaked as I was I made myself calm right the hell down so I could talk to her. "My father, he just collapsed. He just collapsed."

"Is he breathing?" she asked.

I checked him and realized he wasn't. "No." The words barely escaped my lips.

"Has he got a pulse?"

I checked that too and I could have died. "No." Tears started pouring from my eyes. He had no pulse. Dad had no pulse.

How?

I was just talking to him. I was just talking to him.

"Start CPR. I'm sending an ambulance."

It was the hurried tone in the operator's voice that snapped me back and I started the compressions I'd learned in an emergency first aid course.

I pumped but nothing. It didn't stop me. I wouldn't give up on him.

I couldn't.

I was a real mess when the paramedics burst through the door.

Dad was still out cold with no response.

I'd been trying to revive him for five minutes but it felt like it could have been forever.

They didn't waste time they just got on to two rounds of compressions then brought out the defibrillator.

I watched the scene unfold before me in horror.

I couldn't believe this was happening. I couldn't believe what this visit of mine had become.

My father who was not even half an hour ago telling me to find a way to trust Pat and believe in love was on the floor unconscious. Not breathing and his heart wasn't beating.

I continued to watch the monitor every time they seemed to blast him with it. that was the best way I could describe it. blasting his body because the way he shook as they administered the electric shocks was just like that.

I prayed and prayed and prayed he would come back to me.

I prayed and prayed and prayed as I watched.

One of the paramedics looked unhopeful like he wanted the other one administering the shocks to stop.

"Please don't stop. Please." I begged and in my course of begging there was a little beep.

One little beep, then another, and other.

Beep, beep , beep...

His heart came back.

I grabbed my own chest to keep my heart form leaping out.

"We got him back." The paramedic declared and glanced over to me with a nod. "We have to take him in. Does he have any medication?"

"Yes, I'll go get it." I rushed to Dad's room and grabbed all his medicines and everything we'd gotten from dr. Thomson and the community team.

I grabbed what I needed and filled the paramedics in on his medical history on the ride to the hospital.

I didn't know how I was able to be so strong and switch from being weak and freaked out to what Dad needed me to be.

His heartbeat was stable while we were in the ambulance and continued to strengthen. When we got to the hospital the ER doctors took over and my bravado ended.

I was sent to the waiting room to wait and it was there I fell apart.

Alone.

This was what happened to me. I'd had to deal with a lot of major things life had thrown at me all by myself.

When mom left, no one talked about it.

She just left us. Packed her bags one day and left. I watched her pack and she never said anything to me to remember her by. Then Angelica. Me being the little sister foolishly believed my big sister would take care of me. We'd be the glue that kept the family together. Her, me and Dad.

It was not to be so.

She left and had a hand in the stress that made Dad sick.

Now I was here not knowing what was going to happen to him.

I needed air.

Going outside the afternoon breeze hit me and I was able to take out my phone.

Lana was the person I would have called, but she was in Milan.

Her voice would have soothed me, but what I needed was someone to come here and be here with me. Someone to support me and stop me from fading away.

Someone I could rely on to give me some strength.

I found Angelica's number because all of those things I needed should have come from her. She was my sister. I didn't know where she was but she should come here and take care of me.

It was as I went to dial her number that I stopped and came to my senses.

My sister was supposed to be here. She was supposed to give me strength. She should know how sick Dad was, but she wouldn't be the rock I needed right now.

There was only one person in my world that could be that for me.

Only one person my heart had trusted and handed itself to.

One person who loved me enough to do anything for me, because he would never disappoint me.

Pat…

I didn't have to think twice. It was true.

I dialed his number. The phone rang but then went to voicemail.

I pressed the phone close to my ear and left a message.

"Pat, my Dad is in hospital. Please, please come. I need you."

That was all I said and hung up.

Instantly I felt better, even though I never spoke to

him. Even though I knew this morning was shit and I upset him in the worst way.

I trusted him. I did and I knew he would come. No matter what.

He would be here because I needed him.

CHAPTER 26

Patterson

I LOOKED at the glass of whiskey sitting on the counter before me.

It was three in the afternoon and I was sitting in a bar near my house.

I'd come here a few hours ago to drink and try to forget but I found myself just sitting by the counter staring at the large screen TV on the wall watching baseball.

I hated baseball but watching the players provided something to look at.

Something to stare at besides the blank brown wall

in front of me.

I probably should have gone home, but I figured I would have actually hit the bottle hard if I'd done that. That was how I felt. Like I would drown my sorrow in the bottom of the bottle like I used to back in college.

I was wild as it was, me in college was...

Well I didn't know how I survived it. I remembered several instances of getting wasted so bad I couldn't remember what happened the next day or ever. People used to tell me I did stuff and to this day I couldn't remember any of it.

Drunk me loved one thing. Women.

It wasn't all that different to the normal version of me, but I had no control.

That wouldn't work today.

The answer to this morning's debacle was not to get wasted out of my mind and pick up a few easy lays to forget Georgie.

That wasn't the answer and I was sitting here contemplating the one shot of whiskey because I didn't want to do something stupid to make myself look worse.

Here, someone would have to serve me and I'd get a glass at a time.

It was damage control.

I left my phone in the car because I didn't want dad or even Hudson trying my nerves.

I doubted after this morning Hudson would call, but I didn't want to take the risk.

The thing was he was just a bunch of suspicion. No proof because to truly have proof he'd have to hear either myself or Georgie say the words.

It was all fake.

Granted if he was listening in our argument this morning we would have handed him the juice he needed. We would have spilled the tea and the teapot too.

It would have served me right.

Ivan was so wise. He was the kind of guy who could have a good time but keep himself in check.

Me on the other hand I ran with an idea as far as I could. Just because I always got away with some serious shit.

This was the first time I'd gotten caught in the trap. The first time that I screwed myself over and I wasn't sure I could get myself out of it.

Georgie saying no she basically couldn't trust me meant what?

Were we over?

Did it end with those words?

Every time I thought about it my chest tightened and I couldn't get my head around the concept of not being with her. I couldn't see tomorrow without her in my life.

Warm hands brushed over my shoulders. Hands, dainty and feather light like my girl.

For a second I allowed myself to believe that she'd somehow found me. This bar wasn't somewhere I'd go often. I'd been here a handful of times in the past but it wasn't somewhere you'd look for me.

I allowed myself to think that somehow fate guided her to me but I was rudely thrown off course when I looked up and found myself looking at Phoebe.

Her bright blue eyes flickered with mischief. Bright and sinful, stark against her platinum blond hair.

All I needed now was for papers to see me with her and it would be some other scandal.

"Phoebe, hi." I stared at her and tried to make myself look like we weren't together.

"Patterson, it's not your style to be sitting at a bar alone. Where's that fiancée of yours?" She looked me over with pure seduction. There was no question as to what was on her mind.

It grieved me to think that if I were sitting here with Georgie we would have run into her. Phoebe was a woman I hooked up with a couple of times a year.

"She isn't always with me," I answered.

"Hmmmm, so how's this going to work? You haven't said yet. In fact you haven't said anything at all. Are you seriously going to get married and ditch someone like me? That last time we had was very memorable."

It was also an example of why I should never have alcohol. I still couldn't remember all the details of that night.

"Phoebe I'm..."

She leaned closer giving me a good view of the swells of her breasts in that tight top she wore. Seeing her like that would have usually been enough to get me up out of this chair. I would have taken her hand and dragged her someplace private. Didn't matter where that was. My car, my apartment, behind an alley somewhere.

Manwhore...

Manbitch. All Georgie's words. She was right and I had no business being upset because she was simply telling me what she'd seen and knew me to be over the years.

That was all it was.

All truth.

"Come one Pat, let's go somewhere." Phoebe whispered.

I wasn't even tempted and that was the difference in me. I had changed and it wasn't for me to expect Georgie to see it and assume I was serious about her. it was for me to work hard like Ivan said and earn her trust.

It started here.

It started right now.

"Phoebe, I'm sorry. I don't do that anymore. You know I'm engaged. Please respect me, and my girl." I stood up.

Needless to say she looked taken aback, and more shocked as I walked away from her and the drink.

As I stepped outside my mind cleared up some more. I knew what I had to do.

Step one was just now. Walking away from my old life.

Step two was coming clean to Dad no matter the cost.

Step three was winning Georgie over the natural way. I wanted to be sure that when I actually asked her to be my wife and not just mine, she knew that I wanted her to be my soul mate.

I wanted the kind of marriage my parents had. One where we could have forever and still be in love. A marriage where our children could use as an example of what true love was.

Feeling pumped I got to my car and reached for my phone ready to call her. noticed a missed call from her and a voice message.

I listened to it.

"Pat, my Dad is in hospital. Please, please come. I need you." That's what she said.

Panic rose in my throat.

Shit. That message came through two hours ago.

I gunned the engine on my car and sped out of the parking lot. On to step four. Being there for her whenever and where she needed me.

I found her in the ER waiting room crying in the corner all by herself.

I hoped like hell the situation hadn't gotten worse.

When she saw me she threw her arms around me and continued sobbing.

"I'm here, Baby. I'm here." I told her holding her tight and running my hand over her hair. "How is he?"

She pulled back slightly and tried to catch her breath. "He's in surgery. His heart. His heart stopped beating. He needed surgery straight away. They had to replace the valves." She barely managed to explain. "They said the valves were completely damaged. It just got worse over the years."

"Georgie I'm so sorry." It grieved me that her father had been so sick and I didn't know. "Your father is a really strong man. He'll be strong for you."

I knew her father loved her more than life itself and that nothing would keep him from coming back to her. In fact I was banking on it.

"Thank you. Thank you for coming."

"Of course I'd be here." I nodded.

"I knew you'd come. You always come when I need you. Pat I'm so sorry about this morning."

"No, don't apologize. Don't worry about anything. I'm here now and I'll take care of you. You hear me?"

She nodded. "I trust you. I trust you Pat. More than anyone in this world. You were right you never disappoint me."

My spirit soared hearing she trusted me on that level. I cupped her face and gave her a warm smile. "Maybe, it's because my stupid ass was in love with you all that time and I was so dumb I didn't even know."

That was it. That moment when I got the idea to ask her to be part of my crazy plan I did it because there wasn't anyone in this world like her.

I didn't realize at the time that, that was true on all levels.

"Well you know now, and I love you too."

Hearing her say that was the best thing in the world. It was priceless to me.

"Come here." I pulled her back against my chest and kissed the top of her forehead.

I sat with her in the waiting room for the next five hours.

We just waited there for news. Any news good or bad.

At eight the consultant came to speak to us reporting her dad was in a stable condition and the surgery was a success. It was a matter of recovery now and seeing what the next twenty four hours would be like.

We weren't allowed to see him so I just took Georgie home, back to my place.

She tried to stay awake but I could see how drained out she was from the whole day.

She sat in the sofa curled up against one cushion and holding another to her chest.

"I was going to call my sister." She suddenly said. "I don't even know why. She wouldn't have come."

Georgie never spoke about her sister. I knew the details and knew never to really ask too much because she was hurting from her sister's lack of care and absence from her life.

"Maybe one day things will change. Maybe she'll come to you." I offered sitting down next to her.

"No. Today taught me a lot. Today is the last day I think of her and the last day I'll live that life where I'm always scared. I don't want to do it anymore. I don't want to be scared to need people. I don't want to be scared to need you. I don't want to be scared that you wouldn't help me fulfil my dreams. I don't want to be that person anymore. The woman who wants to control everything so she knows what's going to happen."

I was listening. This was the first time she'd opened up to me like this. Expressing her fears.

I took her hands into mine. "Baby steps. One day at a time. One day at a time an I promise you it'll all be okay. Everything."

"Thank you Pat. Dad will pull through, won't he? I don't know what I'd do if he doesn't."

"He will. Let's have faith that he will. Believe he will."

"Believe." She nodded.

"Come let's get you to bed."

"I can't sleep. What if the hospital calls during the night?"

"I left my number for them to call me. if they call I'll answer. Georgie you need to sleep."

"Okay."

I put her to bed and she fell asleep straight away.

I sat by the window watching her and thinking about what I had to do.

This was by no means over yet.

I still had much to do. It was just a matter of getting it done.

I promised her I would take care of her and I would.

I would take care of everything and do this right.

Everything.

I wanted to make it all so she wouldn't have to worry about anything ever again.

CHAPTER 27

Georgie

I WOKE up this morning to find Pat gone. He'd left me a
note to say he was out taking care of a few things. He'd
also called the hospital and was told Dad had woken up.

It was the best news.

I got dressed as quickly as I could and went down to
the hospital where Dr. Thomson greeted me.

"Georgie, I'm glad I got a chance to see you. Can we
talk over here?" He pointed to the corner of the waiting
room that was free of people.

"Sure."

Dad had been moved to one of the wards so this waiting section was a little more comfortable and done up than the ER room.

We went and sat down.

I noticed that Dr. Thomson looked brighter than when I usually spoke to him. I took that as a good sign. I also took it as a good sign that we were talking out here in the waiting room as opposed to in a private office.

"It's good news. Your father should pull through with no trouble. He just needs the extra care. He's asleep now so maybe give him another half an hour before going in the room, and try to limit it to a few minutes at a time. his meds will make him pretty drowsy. But all in all the surgery was a success. It was a lot more invasive than we originally planned because it seemed like the valves just gave up. Replacing them was the better option for him and I'm glad we were able to do so."

"Thank you so much. I'm so grateful. I really am. It was so scary when he fainted. I thought I'd lost him." I couldn't believe that actually happened and it took a defibrillator to revive him and bring him back.

"It pains me to say that you almost did. He's going to be with us for twelve weeks. We'll monitor him here, then move him to a rehabilitation center for an additional four weeks just because he's had a stroke in the past and with the bed rest he's going to need the additional support."

"I'll do whatever he needs. No matter what." I nodded.

"Well we'll do everything in reason. We have all the payment details and I've pushed through your request for a private room once he gets out of ICU."

I narrowed my eyes at him. what did he mean?

Payment detail and request for private room?

I didn't make anything like that, or give any sort of details. I was too distraught yesterday to do all of that and I figured I'd just wait on the bill.

"I haven't left my details yet." I shook my head.

"Well, all your father's treatment has been paid for and we've been instructed to charge anything else to the payment details we have."

I didn't even know why I bothered to be surprised.

Pat.

He did this.

"My God." I knew yesterday was abysmal and would burn an infernal hole in my pocket and possibly my life. I wasn't counting on that two million from Pat. I planned last night not to take it. I couldn't do it anymore.

I didn't want to be paid to love him. That was what

it would always feel like to me so I didn't want it. I would still do all he wanted me to do but I couldn't take the money.

I hadn't thought about the kinks yet but that was as far as I got.

Not taking the money.

Now he'd done this.

It brought me to tears.

"We'll talk more Georgie. Rest assured your father's in good hands. We'll take the best care of him. It's going to be a long road but he'll be stronger for it."

"Thank you, for everything and for being here for us all this time."

He tipped his head and bowed a curt nod then left me.

As I watched him go my thoughts returned to Pat.

Patterson Flynn, you surprise me again.

Surprised and made me crazy. Crazy for him.

Crazy for him in every way possible.

I didn't know what the next few weeks would bring but I was for damn certain going to make sure he knew how much I loved him, and how grateful I was to him.

I waited half an hour and went into see Dad.

He was awake.

He was awake and propped up on a stack of pillows with various tubes running from his arms.

While he looked incredibly weak he still smiled that bright smile he always gave me.

"Baby girl," he said, voice shaky.

"Daddy." I hadn't called him that in years. I rushed up to him and tried to keep myself calm.

"Sweet girl, I got to the tunnel and saw the light. Heck I got to those heavenly gates and told St. Peter I wasn't ready yet because my little girl needed me. I had to come back to walk her down the aisle."

That was it. I couldn't hold the tears back anymore. It didn't take much for me to break down as it was.

"Oh Dad, thank you. thank you for being so strong to pull through. Thank you so much." I was a bunch of thanks.

"Georgia. My dear little girl I'm so sorry I gave you such a scare. You've had to deal with so much. My brave, brave little girl. I'm going to be okay. I promise you I will, I'll be okay and it'll be like it used to be when I could take care of you. Thank God I have some help now." He glanced over my shoulder and I followed his gaze.

Pat stood at the door holding a potted bonsai tree.

He smiled as we looked over at him.

"This was the most manly plant I could get my hands on." Pat said coming in.

"Thanks I love bonsai trees. Good to see you son," Dad beamed at him. "I hear you've been calling almost on the hour since the sun came up."

There was one more thing to make me melt. I couldn't stop looking at Pat.

He glanced over at me. "I wanted to be sure they were taking care of you." pat told him.

"Thanks to you I hear they are." Dad must have known Pat was covering the costs. "I can't thank you enough for looking out for me and my daughter. I'd be real proud to call you my son."

I looked back to Dad and realized something. He'd never judged Pat. Not once. It wasn't like he didn't know what Pat had gotten up to in the past. It was in enough newspapers.

He never once judged him.

"It would be the biggest honor sir, one I wouldn't take lightly."

"I know." Dad nodded. "I *know.*"

"How are you feeling?" "

"Better, stronger in my mind. The body will catch up." dad chuckled. He sounded a little frail again and I remembered Dr. Thomson's caution.

"Dad, we're going to let you rest and come back in an hour or so. I'm just going to be outside."

Dad nodded and his eyelids closed.

I was amazed to see him fall asleep so fast but it was understandable.

Pat took my hand and led me outside back to the waiting area where we sat on one of the padded benches.

I shuffled to face him. "Patterson Flynn." I mused. "I still think your name sounds like a surname, and calling you Flynn would just be rude."

He chuckled. "I was thinking about that a few weeks back. How you think it's better to give me a woman's name rather than call me Patterson."

"Pat doesn't sound like a woman's name when I use it on you."

"I guess not. You always give it that extra attitude, so I know not to try nonsense with you, or any trickery, or funny business."

I just looked at him. "Does this funny business involve paying for my father's treatment?"

He pressed his lips together and tried to suppress a smile.

"It's the least I can do Georgie. There's some stuff I have to talk to you about but first I have something to give you."

My shoulders tensed.

I hated seeing that something was going on and not

knowing what was happening. He looked like he'd done a lot of thinking.

He pulled out an envelope from the inside of his jacket pocket and handed it to me.

"What is this Pat?"

"Something I knew you wouldn't accept lightly, not without having done something first. Something you felt you would have done to earn it."

"Earn? What is it Pat?" I was actually afraid to look.

"It's a sort of redundancy payment. I'm sorry you can't be my PA anymore Georgie. This is bonus payment for Christmas, and the annual staff increase and payment for being you." He chuckled.

I opened the envelope and almost fainted when I saw what was inside.

It was a certificate of ownership for the property on Santa Monica Blvd and next to that was a check. A check for two million dollars.

My gaze snapped to meet his.

"You'll get the title deeds to the property in a few weeks and the other paperwork. I don't think you need to do much else but put the business together." He nodded. "So, you can't work for me anymore. You'll be too busy doing what you should have been doing all this time."

"Pat, I can't. I can't take this. This is so much. It's more than what I ever hoped for in my life." My voice shook as I spoke and my hands trembled. "I haven't done anything."

"You've been everything. It's nothing because you've been priceless to me. please just accept it."

"We didn't get married yet."

A shadow of worry washed over his face and he picked up my hand to gaze at my beautiful, beautiful ring. "I'm calling off the plan Georgie. I'm not doing it. I can't do it. I'm going to tell my father what I did. I've decided that I want you more than I want the Flynn empire."

"*What?*" I couldn't believe what I was hearing.

"You heard me baby, I want you more and because of that I can't let this relationship be based off something fake. It was always real to me. I want to be that man you described. The kind of man you want to share your dreams with, and the next time I ask you to marry me I'm going to ask you to be my wife. I want you to say yes because you want me to be your husband. For real. I'm going to work hard to earn your trust and you won't have to think twice if anyone ever questions whether or not I'm serious about you."

I was shaking so much I couldn't speak.

"Pat..."

"No... You stay here and be here for your Dad. Come home to me if you want or back to yours. I'll check in on you later." He leaned forward and kissed the top of my head.

I just watched him. Watched him smile at me. Watch him love me, watched him walk away down the corridor until he turned the corner and disappeared leaving me with a fortune in my hands.

His words imprinted in my soul.

CHAPTER 28

Patterson

As I walked into Dad's office I was reminded of when I was sixteen years old and I first went to his office to confess. A lot happened when I was sixteen.

Like a sinner going to their priest at confessional, I went to Dad and told him I was the one who crashed his jeep in the lake because I was trying to jump the said jeep over the lake and ended up almost killing myself. I also came clean about lying that a masked car thief had taken it from me, and stole his wallet and spent ten thousand dollars at the casino.

I'd gotten a fake ID and thought I was hot shit.

The reason why I came clean was that the gardeners son was being blamed for taking the car and stealing the money. His mother was our maid at the time and Dad was threatening to fire her and send her son to prison. Her son was eighteen at the time and would have definitely gone inside.

I couldn't allow that to happen. I was about to get away with a big crime I thought was funny, but someone else would suffer for it.

I fessed up and Dad was so mad at me he didn't speak to me for a whole month. When he did start talking to me it was pleasantries. Good morning, good night. hi and bye.

That was it.

I'd embarrassed him in the worst way ever.

I was about to do it again.

This time though I didn't think he would ever forgive me.

I figured what I did was enough to sever our relationship and him to just cut me off for abusing his trust and all around trying to take him for a fool.

No matter what happened, and I supposed it would be bad, I knew I deserved it big time.

I was just glad I had Georgie, or for what I had of her. she was more than what I could ever hope for. My prize.

She was the woman who was my everything and she was more than I deserved coming out of this mess.

Dad looked at me as I stepped into his office.

He smiled and reminded me of Georgie's Dad. It was the kind of smile I thought you'd give your child when you were proud of them.

I'd had every intention of doing this yesterday but I needed more time. just a little bit more time to plan what I was going to say to him.

Georgie came back to me last night but we didn't do much talking.

She tried and I stopped her with a kiss, then I got lost in making love to her.

She was still asleep when I left an hour ago.

"Patterson, people are going to start talking if we keep meeting like this. First thing in the morning meetings are usually of the serious variety." Dad chuckled.

I pulled up the chair in front of him and lowered to sit.

"I just love your face." I joked.

"Oh God, what have you done now? Boy, I'm getting too old for the type of crazy you keep coming up with. I've been running after you for thirty six years."

"I hope you run after me for another thirty six."

"My boy with you anything is possible. I'm sure the good Lord will see it fit to make me live to be a hundred and six to keep you in check."

298

I laughed.

"What's troubling you son?" he asked.

"Dad, I wanted to say thank you for everything. I wanted to thank you for whipping me in shape and showing me what I needed to become. I wanted to thank you for directing my focus so that I could change and be the kind of man a woman like Georgie would want to be with."

"Patterson, you are frightening me right now. I really hope I didn't die . I didn't tell my girl I loved her before I left this morning. The neighbor's cat came in the yard and peed all over her scallions so she was busy with that." Dad shook his head.

I wanted to laugh, that was just the kind of thing Dad would say. He'd called Mom his girl so naturally and so often it was normal for me to hear it. Hearing him say it now warmed my heart. I was grateful that my father was the man he was and loved my mother so much.

"No, Dad you didn't die. I can assure you God wouldn't put me in a room with you with what I have to tell you."

Now he looked really worried. "Now I'm officially panicked. What's up?"

I was about to tell him when a small knock on the door stopped me.

I frowned.

It would be just my luck now if Hudson came in.

Dad held up his hand. "Hold that thought boy, let's see who this is. Can't be that many people who need to see me at nine a.m. sharp. Must be important."

"Yeah." If it was Hudson, I was still going to do it. I would still come clean.

It was just something I promised myself I would do today.

"Come in." Dad called out.

The door opened and Georgie stuck her head in.

She cut me a quick glance and focused on Dad.

Dad face brightened right up. "Pet, good morning."

"Good morning, Mr. Flynn." She gave him her best smile.

"Oh shucks, you're going to have to stop calling me that. *Richard.* Please call me Richard. Or father. Take your pick." Dad chuckled.

"Thank you father," Georgie giggled. "I'm so sorry to disturb you, can I just borrow this husband to be of mine? I promise I won't keep him for too long."

"Certainly."

I waited a moment before I stood. I got up and walked over to her. She took my hand and led me out to the corridor near the fish tank.

Clearly she was here to talk me out of confessing.

"It looks like you haven't told him yet." She tilted her head to the side.

"I was about to Georgie. I have to, I have to tell him. it's the right thing to do."

She smiled, stepped forward and cupped my face to give me a kiss. Then she stepped back and fixed her gaze on me.

"I don't think you have to say anything." She shook her head.

"Why? You know the whole thing is wrong."

"No, it wasn't. Not at all. There was something we kept telling each other this whole time. something we kept saying because it was important. We made sure we both knew it was real. *Real.* It was real for me and I know it was real for you, so what does it matter how it came to be real? It's real no matter what."

I was listening. "Georgie, I don't want you to think of the circumstances of us getting together and think I didn't love you."

She shook her head at me. "No, it's the opposite. You loved me and I loved you. I love you and I have this beautiful ring on my finger you gave me when you asked me to be yours. Even that, you made sure I knew you were speaking from your heart. I said yes then, and I'm telling you now that I want you to be my husband. That's real Pat. It was all real, so you don't have to tell your father anything other than we'll be planning our wedding for as soon as, because I don't want to wait too long to be Mrs. Patterson Flynn."

Not many things could move me to tears. I couldn't remember the last time I cried. Hearing her words however opened up a piece of me that I never thought existed.

I took her hands into mine and she stood on her toes to kiss me and kiss me filling me with the purest joy.

When we pulled apart we noticed someone watching. There was always someone watching.

This time it was the right person.

Down the corridor, completely out of earshot was Hudson.

He gave us a crude stare.

"Let's go home baby." Georgie teased running her finger over my chest and pulling on my tie. "Whip cream and syrup awaits."

I laughed and took hold of her hand.

Whipped cream and syrup were just the start.

I was going to devour this woman forever.

EPILOGUE

Georgie

Six months later ...

I felt just like a princess. A princess dressed in a wedding dress inspired by the nineteen forties. And like we'd been transported right back to that time, Pat and I danced under the stars under the gazebo of our back garden.

We were still dancing , dancing to our wedding song as Mr. and Mrs. Flynn.

It must have been close to two a.m. and we were

supposed to be ready to catch our flight to The Seychelles in five hours but neither of us could bring ourselves to part. To stop dancing to this magical song that we first connected to.

It's Been A Long, Long Time.

It had been because it felt like I'd waited my whole life to meet him and I could honestly say that my life completely changed after I did.

It became exciting, filled with all sorts of adventures, crazy, magical, full of love.

Today had to be a combo of all of that with the culmination of our big day.

On the normal side Dad walked me down the aisle. He was stepping strong now. albeit with a walking stick but the strength behind his strides today showed me how far he'd come.

It was amazing to see our family and friends here. Pat's parents, Lana, Ivan and Jada.

On the adventurous side however was something else.

Or someone else. Someone I never expected to see again.

Angelica.

Pat found her and got her to come to the wedding.

She stayed for the wedding, stayed to congratulate us and then she left before the reception. No hard feelings but she did leave an address and we arranged to meet up with Dad when I got back from my honeymoon.

She looked so embarrassed, but I realized then that I'd rather have her here and in my life than never see her again because of her ability to land herself in trouble.

I was sad to see her go but I accepted it was the way it had to be.

Baby steps.

Tiny steps that would propel me along this path to where ever I was supposed to go.

Pat and I had gotten everything we wanted, but most of all we found each other.

We had each other and instead of my desire to control everything that happened in the future I was happy to stop doing that and allow life to take its course and guide me to wherever it wanted me to be.

I was happy to be spontaneous and take risks.

To live.

As I gazed into my love's eyes I knew I'd never be bored and the rest of forever would be amazing.

Thanks so much for reading and for allowing me to share my stories with you xx

ACKNOWLEDGMENTS

To my readers.
Where would I be without you....
I thank you from the bottom of my heart for all your support,
and for reading my stories.
Hugs and LOVE xx

ABOUT THE AUTHOR

Bella Fontaine is the multicultural and interracial romance pen name of USA Today Bestselling bestselling author Khardine Gray.

The name is to honor the strong, super talented, and courageous women in her family who inspired her to write and do what she loves most.

As with her other books expect hot, steamy, contemporary romance and romantic suspense. Expect drool-worthy heroes and sassy heroines. People falling in love and the wild, sexy fun they have on their journey.

Sign up to her newsletter where you can be spoiled rotten with giveaways and updates on new releases here:

https://www.subscribepage.com/bellafontainebooks

You can find her on Facebook here:
https://www.facebook.com/bellafontaineauthor/

Join the Bliss Romance Hideaway reader group too for
more spoilage and fun:

https://m.facebook.com/groups/889377571219117

Happy reading xx

CPSIA information can be obtained
at www.ICGtesting.com
Printed in the USA
LVHW091340190220
647479LV00001BA/205